A CHARMED MOON

ALSO BY JULIA V. ASHLEY

SHORT STORY COLLECTION
Jazz by Faelight

JULIA V. ASHLEY

A Charmed Moon

A FAERIE MARKET MYSTERY
BOOK ONE

DREAMARC

The story, all names, characters, and incidents portrayed in this production
are fictitious. No identification with actual persons (living or deceased), places,
buildings, and products is intended or should be inferred.

A CHARMED MOON

DREAMARC Press
Madison, Mississippi
dreamarc.com

ISBN: 979-8-9892064-1-4 (hardback)
ISBN: 979-8-9892064-2-1 (paperback)
ISBN: 979-8-9892064-3-8 (ebook)

Cover Photography by Linguist5, Maxborovkov, and Maykal

First Edition: 2025

To Rob Ashley
My beacon in the dark

Chapter 1

SABINE

A breeze off the Mississippi River washed the stench of liquor and sweat clear, leaving a slow cooked roux of Creole spices. Souls bled from the bricks as century old buildings wriggled, settling into one another. Brightly colored shutters were thrown open, releasing murmured conversations. And the stately oaks of Jackson Square drowsed in front of St. Louis Cathedral.

Locals and tourists alike took on an electric charge. These crisp fall months promised crackling wraiths stretching their old bones inside the city's cemeteries. Ghost tours went from frivolous fantasy to eerie certainty.

Across the Big Easy, you could feel the dead awake.

Sabine stretched out her lithe fox form to capture as much of the magic as possible. Her father had sent her from their bayou home to live with her aunt near the Greenwood Cemetery in New Orleans. He'd hoped the older witch would teach his daughter how to wrangle the magic simmering in her blood before it exploded, or so he said. But Sabine knew her abilities were too thin to cause any trouble. She hadn't wanted to come, but she had. And found her aunt dead.

She'd been surviving on her own since, piecing together bits of magic as she was able. Most of the spells she knew were cobbled together on the spot and under duress. But a few tricks here and there were enough to keep her fed and occupied. She could feel the magic leeching from the buildings, the streets, and even the river. But she could only catch glimpses of it now and then.

The only other creatures she'd met who knew anything about magic were the crew she'd helped send to jail for the murder of her aunt. The other person, decidedly non-magical and most definitely grumpy, didn't believe in people like her and was perfectly content in his ignorance.

But she wasn't lonely, she told herself. Not really.

Just hungry.

Spotting a young man approaching, she melted into the shadow of a cast iron balcony and reverted back to her true self: a petite woman with an auburn ponytail and matching velvet jumper and slippers.

She wasn't a true shifter, more of an effortless thief.

Sabine initially stole fox form only when frightened, but she'd soon learned to do it out of convenience. A talent the other Domingue witches hadn't possessed, as far as she knew. Which wasn't very far. Fox form allowed her to get into and out of more spaces more quickly than her true form. And sometimes, traveling as a wild animal, even in a big city, was safer than moving about as a young woman alone.

The approaching man had the lazy gate of a tourist mid-visit, one who'd found the rhythm of the city, but was not yet desperate to snatch up the last strands of magic before going back to wherever they'd left. He gave Sabine a sensual smile.

She ducked her chin and studied the man through her lashes. His slow blink looked as if he'd skipped the CBD store in the riverboat casino in favor of a back alley distributor. When he was close enough to speak but didn't, Sabine returned his smile with the shy, quiet smile of a girl who wanted more than she dared.

As they passed, the stranger ran a hand down her bare arm, and Sabine leaned into it, briefly resting her hand on the waistband of his low-slung jeans. Then they parted, knowing the brief interaction would be no more than a vague memory by morning.

Sabine turned the corner down Magazine Street and slipped the young man's wallet, newly liberated from his back pocket, into her leather satchel. As usual, this put a skip in her step. She reveled in the ease of life as a sneak thief on the streets of the Big Easy. Two more blocks, and she cut back north, zigging and zagging her way through the gridded streets.

At the next turn, a familiar baritone startled her to a stop. A quick check of her satchel assured her that all the zippers were zipped and all the evidence out of sight. Ahead, a gaggle of police officers radiated out from a central figure. A man with a stern yet handsome face. A bold figure with broad shoulders encased in a rather sad, sagging suit jacket which had given in to the afternoon's humidity. He doled out orders to the men and women in uniform in that rumbly voice she remembered from the time she was on the receiving end of it.

Twenty or so officers blocked the entrance to a building. Tired but proud, it loomed behind them, with a pitted stucco base and kiln fired brick rising two more stories to the roof. The eagerness of the officers decreased with the increase in their age. The oldest checked his watch and shook his wrist as if that might help it keep time a little faster. The youngest bristled with enthusiasm, his eyes wide and alert as his hand twitched towards his utility belt.

The barked orders came from the one in the middle, a tall Cajun man with a determined scowl. He surveyed the officers, nodded, and dismissed them to their duties. Leaving him alone under the cast iron awning. And leaving Sabine with a delightful opportunity.

"Detective Jean-Luc Thibodeaux," she crooned. "How lovely to see you again."

The man's attention snapped to her as she flowed down the sidewalk with the confidence of a robin hectoring a hawk. Officers swerved aside to avoid colliding as Sabine walked a straight line toward her prey.

Seeing that at least two of the younger officers loitered to observe, Sabine cocked her head and gave the detective a coy blink of her lashes. Detective Thibodeaux grimaced, ducked his head, and flipped open a notepad, but not quick enough to hide a twitch at the corner of his mouth.

Delightful. Sabine could still get under his defenses.

"Ms. Domingue, what are you doing in these parts?"

"Oh, Jean-Luc. We're practically old friends. Why be so formal? Sabine will do."

"It's *what* she'll do that concerns me," he muttered in a voice pitched for her alone.

Her cheeks ached with the force of her triumphant grin. He did remember her. She stopped toe-to-toe with the detective, her auburn velvet slippers touching his well-polished black boots. Thibodeaux stood a head taller than her, so she had to tip her head back in order to meet his gaze.

Letting out a slow sigh, Thibodeaux flipped his notebook shut and turned to face the building's entrance. Sabine snickered. Neatly done. He'd deftly executed the smooth maneuver, distancing himself from her without actually backing away.

A female officer approached, but Thibodeaux efficiently redirected her with fresh orders before speaking to Sabine again.

"I have work to do here. If you've come to turn yourself in for petty thievery or accidental manslaughter, I'm sure Officer Wilhelm would be more than happy to help you." With a tip of his head, the detective indicated a man in uniform looking through the trunk of a police cruiser. His relaxed, efficient manner gave him away as a veteran of the force.

Sabine turned to face the entrance as well, with her arm pressed against his. "First of all, there's nothing petty about me. Second of all, if I slaughtered a man, it would not be an accident."

Without responding, Thibodeaux abandoned her on the sidewalk and entered the building. Sabine huffed and sprinted to keep up. When the detective discovered her on his heels, he jerked to a stop, shook his head, and pointed back to the door.

"This is a crime scene."

"Ooh, yes. And we make such an excellent crime-fighting duo."

Thibodeaux closed his eyes and took a deep breath. He remained that way long enough that Sabine imagined he was counting to ten before addressing her again. She'd barely wiped the smirk from her face when he did. "We are not a duo. I am a detective, and you are . . . not. Please, leave."

Sabine's shoulders dropped, her triumphant grin drooped, and she twirled on the toes of her slippers to face the door. Pausing with a hand on the brass doorknob, Sabine listened for the ring of the elevator opening and the whoosh of it closing before turning back around.

There Thibodeaux stood, arms crossed.

"Go."

"I'm gone," Sabine gave an impertinent bobble of her head and left.

Chapter 2

MEGAN

The sun, fat and happy from a lazy day crossing the cloudless sky, sank into the clutches of the oaks standing guard over Café du Monde. The Mississippi River let out a cool sigh of relief as the cruise ships pulled away from the riverwalk and drifted towards the Gulf of Mexico.

Relieved of the afternoon sun, people flowed into and out of the café for their pre or post dinner beignets. The warm smell of fried yeasty bread, liberally coated in powdered sugar, did its best to cover the loamy fish odor stirred up as the ships passed by. Two college grads, Megan Armand and her old roommate and current apartment mate, Valdi, bided their time in the long lines behind sweaty dads, holding the hands of wriggling kids and bedraggled moms carrying whining babes.

Everyone in their twenties must be stowed away in restaurants eating before a long night of drinking. Or closed up in air-conditioned rooms, saving their money in preparation for that same night. Meg wanted to show off as much of New Orleans their first weekend as she could. And Café du Monde was a must. Or it had been when she was one of those wriggling kids clinging to her older brother's hand.

Now, Meg stood a head taller than most of the tourists. It gave her an advantage in keeping track of Valdi, a compact woman composed all of curves and curiosity. If Meg lost sight of her, the short woman would disappear into the crowd—off examining a group of people with peculiar accents, or a tour group taking in the century-old stories, or even a single stranger that she thought might bear further investigation.

Meg tried to reign her in, wanting to stuff all the best of New Orleans into a single evening. That could not be done by chasing peculiarities. There were simply too many.

The air tasted sweet from the fog of sugar and sweat emanating from the open-air café. The line snaked alongside the low metal fence erected to separate those who had their food and were lucky enough to find a table, and those who huddled under the sliver of shade provided by the overhang.

Beignets for dinner were a sound choice. Then, they could spend the next few hours touring the French Market while the club scene got geared up. Or so she told Valdi, demonstrating how a veteran of the city planned their day.

Slowly, they made their way to the front of the sugar frosted line and collected their fried and dusted treats. Meg made the same futile attempt as all Café du Monde patrons before her. She attempted to delicately eat hers without a mess. However, the sheer amount of sugar exceeded what could be successfully adhered to one pastry by the residual oil. White powder feathered down over her wrists, her forearms, her turquoise tank top. There was no way but through in such a dire situation.

Meg and Valdi were a study in contrasts.

Meg, tall and lanky, stretched out like a taffy, had grown up in the nearby town of Abita Springs to want-to-be hippy parents who had missed the height of their intended era by a couple of decades. She'd struggled her way toward stoic respectability, but failed. Due in large part to her impulsivity, she'd missed her intended goal more remarkably than her parents had missed theirs.

Her one success toward reasonable levelheadedness had come as a collegiate coincidence when the University of Memphis paired her with Valdi for a roommate during their undergraduate studies. Valdi earned a degree in psychology and a minor in applied behavioral analysis. Meg still had no idea what that meant. She'd gotten her degree in English with a concentration in literature. Which everyone understood to mean she would never find a job.

Stable, dependable, practical Valdi pinched her beignet between thumb and forefinger as she analyzed Meg's efforts at conquering the pastry. The same expression on her face that she wore when studying everything Meg did. Like a complex experiment doomed to fail, with only the narrowest possible margin for success.

Valdi had always studied humanity like a sociology experiment gone awry. It made Meg self-conscious, but this was her turf, and she was determined to show the Chicago native how to live in the sultry southern city. She brushed the powder from her shirt, leaving a streak of white fingerprints across her breast.

New Orleans wasn't exactly Meg's turf, but it was close enough. Abita Springs was a small community an hour north, across Lake Pontchartrain. Well, even though she claimed Abita Springs, she'd actually grown up about twenty minutes east in a small gathering of homes built in a generous clearing in the woods of Louisiana.

Some might call it a commune, but *community* does not necessarily mean *commune* or *cult*. She'd argued this point several times over the past two years with her big city roommate. And she wasn't sure if she'd ever truly convinced Valdi it wasn't a backwoods attempt at a cult.

Her mother brought her and her two brothers into New Orleans in January when it was bearable to be outside watching the minor parades leading up to Mardi Gras. She'd made all her kids swear they would not go into the city the weekend of the big celebration held in February. Two of the three had broken that oath as soon as they had friends with cars. To her shame, Meg was the one who hadn't.

Maybe her lack of friends had been the cause of her overly responsible nature.

But no more.

Meg had convinced Valdi to transfer to Tulane for her graduate degree so that they could share an apartment in downtown New Orleans. This weekend's goal, other than impressing Valdi, was to find a job to go with their apartment. And that meant getting over to the marketplace.

Sucking her fingers clean, Meg motioned for Valdi to get on with it. "Eat up. We'll tour the square, then wander down the riverwalk."

"You said you wanted to visit the French Market. Won't it be closed soon?"

"This is New Orleans. Nothing closes before midnight." Meg pointed to the café sign showing it stayed open until 1am.

"You're going to attempt to get a job looking like you've been mauled by a mime?" Valdi pointed to the white fingerprints tracked across Meg's left breast.

She shrugged it off as if such small things as the mark of the mime on your chest didn't matter here. "Perfect, because today we're incognito as tourists."

"We *are* tourists."

"We moved everything into the apartment. That makes us residents. I'm just scoping out job opportunities tonight. Working after dark at the market leaves my days open for cultural studies." Meg was trying to convince her roommate that she could get a second master's through an independent studies program. Valdi seemed about as convinced of that possibility as she was of Meg not being an ex-cult member.

"Working in a bar would do the same."

"In a bar, you only get to see two types of people. Drunk or looking to get drunk. The market has a mix of everyone from everywhere. You'll see."

"Unless it's closed."

"Nothing in New Orleans closes before midnight," Meg repeated with all the confidence of someone who had no idea what they were talking about.

Chapter 3

SABINE

The young female officer returned with police tape. Giving Sabine the side-eye, the woman entered the building and punched the elevator button. When it didn't immediately open, she reverted to the stairs.

Good. Much easier to follow.

Four apartments lined the musty corridor. Its wainscoting molted heavy layers of paint, and the dark floorboards creaked from fatigue. The officer let herself into apartment 201 just to the left of the stairs. As the apartment's door lazily creaked closed, Sabine wedged her auburn slippered foot into the opening.

The tap of the inattentive officer's hard-soled shoes faded inside. Sabine peered around the doorframe. The living and dining areas were empty. So, she saw fit to let herself in.

As she crossed the threshold, a noxious odor turned Sabine's stomach and caused her eyes to water. Once inside, the offending smell evaporated. A warped film wavered across the opening. It began to pulse in time with her heartbeat and expanded toward her.

Stumbling back, she tripped over the arm of a couch and sat hard on the sagging cushions. With her feet in the air, she peered over the back of the couch. The door appeared as innocent as any doorway in a hundred-year-old building in New Orleans, which was to say, not completely blameless but not malicious.

No, film. No pulse. No odor. But a bitter taste remained on her tongue.

Luckily, there was also no one in the room to see her awkward shamble to roll over and off the couch. The moment had come and gone in an instant without drawing anyone's attention.

The small apartment aspired to the shabby-chic with hardwood floors and tall windows. But its furniture missed the mark by several years of hard use. It had a sagging, comfortable vibe, but sparse enough to feel melancholy and lonely. Or maybe she was just projecting her life onto it.

Voices came from the bedroom. So, Sabine gave it a wide berth as she made a slow circuit of the outer room.

A Roku flashed frantically in the console beneath a flat-screen TV, urgently attempting to alert the inhabitants that it no longer had a signal. A retro-looking turntable sat on a shelf with no records in sight. A tan pet bed rested on one end of the sofa, filled with matted, short, black hair. Unopened bills covered one end of a glass top dining table. The rest was covered by unfolded laundry, creating a crescent around the one bare spot, splattered with crumbs, drippings, and moisture rings.

The tiny galley kitchen had dirty dishes piled in the sink and pots stacked on the sliver of a counter beside it. A glance in the fridge showed no edible food, but two unopened bottles of water. Taking one, Sabine swished a mouthful and then downed the bottle to replenish the moisture she'd sweated off while traversing the tourist district earlier in the day.

How dare the detective dismiss her. It's not as if his officers were up to the job, letting Sabine wander in. He was lucky she was here to reveal their ineptitude.

Lucky for him and potentially an exciting evening of crime drama for her. Sabine had no intention of letting the detective steal this from her. She assured herself it was morbid curiosity and not Thibodeaux that attracted her to the crime scene.

Although tormenting him was such fun.

Thibodeaux desperately needed her help, even if he wasn't willing to admit it. He would never have solved the Fortier murders without her. A dangerous drug ring that threatened the lives of the law-abiding citizens of New Orleans.

Sabine snickered. The citizens of New Orleans weren't necessarily known for abiding the law. Fortier had formed a gang of creatures to help him deal drugs and death. Thibodeaux had caught the fastidious gentleman crook and his pack of shifters thanks to her. If she hadn't thrown herself into the middle of his shifter thugs, Fortier would still be dealing death through the Fairy Dust from upriver.

It wasn't as if Sabine didn't believe Thibodeaux was good at his job. Certainly, a man with such a convincing scowl had to be at least mildly competent. But he could *not* do what *she* could do.

Really, she could barely do what she had done, but she was learning. It wasn't easy teaching yourself magic, whether you were born to it or not. Her mother was gone. Her aunt was gone. And here she was, the last of the Domingue Coven.

With a wary glance at the offending door to the corridor, Sabine strolled into the bedroom with the second bottle of water.

Detective Thibodeaux huddled with two officers in front of an open wardrobe. The first, the woman who was generous and inattentive enough to allow Sabine inside the crime scene. The second, a middle-aged officer. Ignoring them, Sabine examined the items strewn across the top of a chest of drawers. A scratched, open-faced pocket watch disappeared into the pocket of her jumper. The rest remained untouched.

It wasn't until she reached the windowsill, with its wilting variegated fern and depleted succulent, that Sabine's presence was finally noticed. These government employees were certainly lacking in spatial awareness.

"Sabine."

She glanced over her shoulder at the two startled officers and one very surly detective. "Yes?"

"Excuse us, please," Thibodeaux said, and the officers immediately disappeared into the outer room. He raised an eyebrow at the water bottle. She tipped it toward him. He shook his head wearily. A spark of guilt almost ignited, but Sabine successfully squelched it.

"I told you—you know what? Forget it. I have a mind to arrest you."

Sabine took a swig of water as she joined him in front of the wardrobe to speak conspiratorially. "We really need to have a discussion about the proficiency of your staff. I find it lacking."

"What I want," he began, but paused to remove an AirPod charger from Sabine's hand and return it to the nightstand, "is for you to understand this is a police matter. If I need to have you bodily removed, I will."

"Ooh, would you be handling me yourself?" she said, rubbing her shoulder against his biceps. This time, he did take a step back. "Come on, I have talents. I could be useful."

His lips tightened as if ready to call for her removal, but he hesitated. A furrow formed in his brow as he studied her. "Maybe you can be of use. Before I have you frisked, then thrown out." He added the latter as he went into the adjoining bathroom.

In the narrow space, he turned in a tight circle with one hand out. "Do you smell that?"

Sabine sniffed. Something burned her nose. She could decipher smells best in fox form, but this was not the time to remind him of her wilier ways. As if he would forget. Although, he might've if he were as clueless as his officers.

"Burnt hair and oils?" Sabine said absently as she rummaged through the medicine cabinet.

Thibodeaux shut the mirror, barely missing her fingertips. He didn't look contrite in the slightest. "Yes. Do you think it could be some . . . I don't know, attempt at a spell or something?"

Attempt. Despite what he'd seen in the past, the detective was still determined to believe in a world without the chaos of magic. Poor dear. Sabine almost felt sorry for him. But he'd grown up in the Big Easy. He really had no excuse for such ignorance.

"More likely, it's beard balm and a beard straightener."

"Straightener?" Thibodeaux looked skeptical.

"Is it really easier to believe in spooky spells than a little manscaping?"

"I'm not sure that's what manscape—" Sabine let him squirm as he stumbled over explaining the definition to her. When he apparently decided he couldn't, or wouldn't, she stepped in again to help.

"Some men like a tidy beard. They're not all Neanderthals." The detective's hand reached for his own chin, but he stopped it short. "Don't be self-conscious. Your clean shave is quite becoming."

"I think we're done. Carmichael," Thibodeaux called, and the female officer promptly arrived. Thibodeaux had the nerve to have the officer pat Sabine down, and the woman had the audacity to look smug about it.

"Should I search her satchel?" she asked.

Thibodeaux shook his head. "You can leave on your own, or I can have Carmichael walk you down."

The officer narrowed her eyes at Sabine.

"I know the way. I'll show myself out while you give your staff that competency lecture, we discussed." Sabine sauntered out of the room. Before leaving, she searched the doorway for any signs of sentience, but it played dumb.

She attempted to push her meager magic at it, and was pleasantly surprised to find she could. Her fingers tingled as her magic brushed against the door frame. Although she'd learned to control a transformation into fox form, magic rarely came at her bidding.

Her excitement swelled at this small victory, and the traitorous magic fizzled out. Dumping her like a bad date. Fine. She didn't need it, anyway.

Holding her breath, she stepped through and was rewarded by a sharp electrical snap, leaving the bare skin of her arms stinging.

She rubbed off the shock and yelled back inside.

"Jean-Luc, you might want to see to this veil attached to the door before you leave. It seems pretty suspicious to me. And potentially dangerous."

That got their attention. Rushed steps thudded across the floorboards, headed her way. But Sabine made sure she was gone before anyone reached the corridor.

Frisk me and throw me out. I hope it zaps your ass.

Chapter 4

MEGAN

While Café du Monde promised to remain open and serving sticky pastries for hours to come, streetlights blinked themselves awake all along Decatur Street. Meg and Valdi flowed against the tide of pedestrians. Behind the café, block after block of storefronts stretched, yawned, and shuttered themselves off to the public.

"Those are just the shops. The French Market will be open," Meg insisted, her long legs outpacing her roommate's. When she realized Valdi was dragging behind, she stopped and anxiously bounced on the balls of her feet in front of the sleepy facades. "Come on, we need to catch them before they pack up."

To her credit, the unflappable Valdi did break into a jog, but even that was slow by Meg's standards.

As they reached the portion of the market that nested under a steel colonnade, rolling carts filled with boxes streamed out like ants from a kicked ant pile. Meg plunged under the canopy, unwilling to believe that anything closed in New Orleans before midnight. Yet lights snapped out one after the other under the branching canopy as vendors packed up their tables. Most were already empty.

She groaned in exasperation, turning in a circle, hunting for vindication. Her muscles drew tight like a spring, while

Valdi stood beside her, posture loose and at ease. Her lack of surprise at Meg's impulsivity ruining plans, yet again, twisted her tension higher.

A head popped up from behind a table she hadn't noticed on her way in. A sharp-toothed grin wore a groove into a pinched face with equally sharp eyes. "What lovely ladies. What suits your fancy this evening?"

Meg looked down on the vendor, barely taller than his display. "Is the market shutting down?"

"One shuts down. One opens up. It is the way of the In Between." His grin grew wider so that Meg feared its corners might spike his ears. "You must harbor a deep desire to find your way here. Perhaps I can satisfy it."

He waved a gnarled hand over his gilded goods. Tables of dazzling jewelry surrounded him. Light from the lanterns overhead danced within gemstones dangling from gold chains or set in polished silver filigree. His wares appeared in starbursts and crescent moons, dragonflies and beetles, toadstools and ornate trees.

How had she passed the booth without seeing it? It must all be fakes, or he'd sell his goods in one of the shops instead of spread out on tables like in a bazaar.

Colorful crystal sparked, and Meg flinched. She nearly missed the sly curve of the man's grin. Valdi paid the odd man no notice. A pair of amethyst orbs dangled from her fingers on delicate silver chains. The stones glowed, reflecting violet in her normally ice-blue eyes.

Meg bumped her elbow. Valdi seemed to snap out of a trance, but instead of noting Meg's signal that they should get away from this creepy dude. Valdi instead addressed that creepy dude.

"How much for these?"

The man's eyes crinkled. "Oh, those are not for sale."

"Of course they are," Meg snapped, then fumbled a rationale for her irritated tone. "You're a vendor, right? And these are your, like, goods and stuff. Of course, you're selling them."

Valdi's attention stayed on the vendor, eager. "Twenty dollars? Two hundred?" He turned his back on the two of them, and Valdi's face fell. Her grip on the earrings tightened.

Around them, the market came to life. Booths were again filled with colorful scarves and capes and dresses. Others had delicate glistening wings hanging from mid-air from invisible strings. Fireflies flickered on and off between them, their light sending staccato messages through the transparent fabric. Still, others had gruesome masks of leering beasts, varnished black with curling horns and snarling snouts.

New Orleans could cater to the most extreme human interests. You really can buy anything here, but Meg remembered more ordinary booths. Vendors with multi-colored sarape and cheap plastic jewelry. Maybe those booths were deeper into the market with less traffic.

A woman in an auburn jumper with a matching ponytail flowed through the growing crowd of customers. Her movements were light and fluid, like that of a dancer. She brushed up against Valdi, who hung the amethyst earrings onto a tree of spiraling black wire. It supported jeweled butterfly clips, enameled flower pins with delicate geared bees, and earrings dangling like ripe fruit. The woman whispered in

Valdi's ear as if they were old friends, and Valdi nodded solemnly.

"Excuse me," Meg said loud enough for the woman to hear over the growing din.

The woman took no notice as she stroked the limbs of the brilliantly bedecked tree. When she walked away, the earrings were no longer hanging from the limb.

The grimacing face of the vendor swung around. "You, witch, you hear me?" he called after the woman. "Wretched thief, you know the rules of the market. I report you, and your access is terminated.

The auburn woman glided along the edge of the table, languidly sliding her hand over the jewelry as if taunting him. He rose to the bait and ran along the table after her, shouting curses until she reached the end. As she moved on to the next booth, she tossed a sparkling collar, like a bouquet built of a myriad of jewels, over her shoulder. The man jumped to catch the necklace and clutched it to his chest, muttering a litany of curses under his breath.

Valdi watched the woman walk away while stroking the curls around her face, a nervous habit of hers. Her only nervous habit as far as Meg knew.

"Hey, you," said the gnarled little vendor.

Startled to realize he was addressing her, Meg tried to form a snappy retort, but what ended up coming out was, "What?"

Very clever.

"Take this and be gone with you," he held out a gold chain bracelet. "Take it. Possess it. It's yours. And be gone."

"But I, well," Meg wasn't sure she wanted to deal with such an unpleasant fellow. But something about the bracelet charmed her. "I really don't need anything, thank you." She turned to go, but he caught at her sleeve.

"You'll need it to hold your charms."

"Oooh, a charm bracelet." Valdi's face lit up again. She normally didn't wear any jewelry. So, Meg was surprised at her interest. Her roommate stopped playing with her hair, took the chain from the vendor, and drop into Meg's palm.

"It's not a charm bracelet," Meg said. "There are no charms."

"I provide the links. I leave it to others to provide the charms. Now take your little friend and pester someone else." He still clutched the jeweled collar, his shoulders curled in around it, as if protecting it from further theft.

"Well, how much?" she stammered.

"Your absence is payment enough." He jerked his chin for them to be gone.

"I'm not a thief," Meg insisted, thinking of the auburn woman.

"Did I say you were a thief? I do not deal with thieves. Take it. Go. The Fae will have their way with you, one way or the other. You might as well have a memento to record the damage done. It's not as if you'll remember on your own." The vendor turned his back to them and ducked under the table. He rose a moment later at the opposite side of the booth without the necklace. He must have stashed it somewhere safe.

"What an odd little man," Meg muttered to Valdi as the vendor attended to another customer. A delicate male with a gaunt face and long, slender fingers caressed a burnished copper cuff with etchings along its edge. The vendor leaned in, his smile unnaturally large.

Valdi took Meg's wrist and slid the bracelet on. Her palm tingled as the chain crossed it and settled just below her wrist bones. She wanted to protest, but once the bracelet lay against her skin, she couldn't imagine removing it.

"Well, he did say take it and leave."

"And leaving was the payment." Valdi took her hand and tugged her down the aisles between the busy booths.

Firelight flickered from the sconces. It reflected off the wares of a neighboring table. The light cut Meg's vision so that she couldn't see what they were selling. Across from it, another booth sucked in the light, swallowing it whole. A gaping void remained where the next vendor would be.

Meg picked up her pace. She turned to see if Valdi was keeping up on those short legs when she noticed a delicate purple glow between Valdi's golden curls.

"Valdi, are those—"

"The fox gave them to me," she said, touching the earrings.

"What fox?" Meg asked.

In answer, an auburn red fox darted between a man's legs. His calves were oddly twisted and his boots were twisted. He looked disturbingly as if he had goat's legs. Busy staring, Meg was nearly run down by a broad man with a scowl shoving people aside in a vain attempt to catch the fox.

This was all very strange, even by New Orleans standards. Valdi didn't seem to share her concern. Her eyes were alight with curiosity. Her mouth was tight with excitement. She looked as if she might dive in and start investigating every oddity. Disassembling each puzzle like a particularly intriguing piece of machinery.

As she swayed toward a booth with tapestries closing it off from view, Meg caught her arm.

"Come on. We're getting out of here."

Chapter 5

THIBODEAUX

Detective Jean-Luc Thibodeaux ushered everyone out of apartment 201, one of four units on the floor. He instructed Carmichael to follow everyone down and make sure they had their orders before leaving. Sweeping his gaze over the apartment a final time, he nodded to himself and locked up.

The lab techs were efficient. The officers here were capable, mostly. Carmichael and a couple of others made up for those just counting the hours until their weekend started. They had all the information they were likely to get here, which was likely not enough to find this guy if he didn't want to be found.

Yet, something about this case felt off.

People went missing every day. The port city was a perfect jumping off place for anyone who wanted to disappear. Hide on one of the barges going downriver to the Gulf. Hop a train, easier done than it ought to be. Leave on I10 in a borrowed car, in the driver's seat, or the trunk. Both worked depending on whether the disappearance was your idea or not.

The young man in question, a Mr. Tyler Davis, had recently moved to town, rented the apartment a couple months past, and was reported missing by family. Surely a runaway or stow away or kidnapping. Had to be. But it didn't *feel* like it.

It felt *charged*.

You're letting that petite pickpocket get to you, he told himself.

Sabine was not an investigator, but she did have skills that could be useful. Turning into a fox didn't count as law enforcement expertise, but it did get her into some unusual situations. He'd seen the transformation himself, but still couldn't believe it. In the middle of the night, waiting for sleep and watching his bedroom ceiling fan's mesmerizing cycle, he'd tried to deny what he'd witnessed, but morning always came without an answer.

His first encounter with the clever woman came while investigating a murder. Led by a raucous crow, Jean-Luc had followed a trail of glittering dust, a new drug from upriver, to an abandoned building. Sabine had been hiding there since finding her aunt murdered. Jean-Luc had investigated that murder. One of his first, and he'd written it off as an overdose.

The memory still grated. He'd been unwilling to see anything he didn't consider natural. He was trying hard to break that habit. Too many *un*natural things happened in New Orleans for him to ignore them all and still do his job.

Sabine had helped. She'd led him to the evidence to convict a drug gang, but she'd put her own scrawny hide on the line to do it. No matter how clever she thought she was, or how much he begrudgingly agreed with her on that point, she was not trained for this kind of work. The only thing he knew her to be trained in was petty theft.

What made him ignore every instinct he possessed around her?

Sabine was impulsive, unpredictable, and a danger to herself. And he didn't know how she could get under his skin so easily. But she'd been right before about the magical end of things. Even now, no matter how much evidence to the contrary, he was reluctant to accept it as a plausible option.

It went against all his training, against every carefully honed instinct. He tried, but he was a detective, damn it. He could only rely on what he could see and hear and touch. And you can't touch magic.

Jean-Luc knew because he'd looked for it. So, he'd keep denying it, until the mountain of evidence fell over and crushed him, probably.

Trotting down the stairs, he let his mind circle back to Sabine's warning.

What veil had she been talking about? Was she just screwing around with him? Sabine might be a crafty thief and a shameless flirt, but he hadn't known her to lie.

Carmichael had gone over the doorway twice under his watch and found nothing out of the ordinary. No sign of anything *witchy* or supernatural. Except that first step into the apartment, he remembered. A quick snap had left the back of his neck stinging, and he'd had the odd taste of burnt boudin on his tongue ever since.

Was that magic? Or just a mosquito and a stale apartment left without AC for a week?

Troubled by the thought, Jean-Luc exited the building, reached into his pocket for his keys, and felt something smooth and round. He pulled out a silver pocket watch with a scratch across the cover.

"Damn it."

He knew the watch from photos he'd directed Carmichael take of the apartment's contents. He searched the street for any sign of that foxy pickpocket.

That did it. Sabine was toying with him. There was no veil. He'd let her cloud his thinking. That's another reason he did not need her on the scene. She could not or would not take it seriously.

As much as he loved the city, New Orleans had its ugly underside. It was infested with petty thieves like Sabine, but it also hid more monstrous characters who would chew up and swallow someone like her. She might act all street wise, but she wasn't born here. She didn't know the streets like he did.

"You have got to get that woman out of your head," he warned himself. "You know what she is. Why do you let her get away with contaminating a crime scene?"

"What's that, sir?" Carmichael joined him at the police cruiser. He tossed her the keys.

"You take the car back. I want to check on something upstairs. Try to get the samples to the lab before it closes. I'd like a report back tomorrow, if possible."

She hesitated. She'd been around him long enough to know how thorough he was. The chance of him forgetting something was slim. He gave her a curt nod, and she rounded the car. "You want me to swing back by and pick you up?"

"No, I'll walk. Give me a chance to think." This wasn't the first time he'd said that. Carmichael knew when to give him space to think, and she knew walking was how he broke thoughts loose. He watched her pull away from the curb, then headed back to the apartment to return the watch.

Muttering about unwanted distractions. He climbed the stairs.

The wood-paneled door of apartment 201 looked no different from any of the other apartments. He placed his hand flat on the door. No zap of electricity. It wasn't until he turned the key that he felt it. A tug as the tumbles of the lock turned. A force pressing against his hand, as if the air around the lock resisted his action. The brass knob buzzed in his hand, and a tingle went up his arm.

Had that happened before?

Don't let her plant false evidence in your head. Snap out of it.

Despite his self-scolding, he moved cautiously. A smart detective always did. Pushing the door open, Jean-Luc examined the frame before crossing over. It looked as innocent as before. No intricate webs of magical light to catch him. No mysterious glow.

The sun sank behind the buildings across the street. The room was dark until the street lamps ignited to cut yellow rectangles of light on the wall. Everything appeared exactly as he'd left it, a bachelor pad with little to no evidence of what happened to its owner.

"Stop conjuring mysteries where they don't exist."

Yet he hesitated. Maybe he should call for Carmichael.

No, then he'd have to explain why he had the watch in his pocket and who'd put it there. It was much easier to fool himself into believing Sabine was not actually a thief if he didn't put the evidence out for others to see.

Realizing he'd tensed his shoulders for impact, he grunted in annoyance and ordered himself to relax, which only ever works marginally, at best.

"Stop stalling."

Jean-Luc stepped across the threshold and began screaming up blood.

Chapter 6

SABINE

Energy sparked and crackled in the French Market after dark as it left its human patrons and courted the uncanny. When it became the Faerie Market of New Orleans. A magical affair with a Creole flavor. A lyrical tune told through the brass of a saxophone, which evolved into spellbound jazz.

The zing of ethereal electricity zapped Sabine's skin, causing her rich auburn fur to rise. It tweaked her nose and dazzled her eyes so that her senses could not be depended upon to lead her through the labyrinth of booths out to the misty air and safety. It made robbing the vendors a risky business, better suited to a creature from the Beyond and not a simple Domingue witch who happened to trip into fox form.

Not a safe pursuit.

She could end up skinned and stretched and put on display as a mask with her soul looking through the glass eyes they'd use to replace hers. Or trapped in one of the filigree cages that hung from hooks, waiting for a creature such as herself. Left spinning on display, she wouldn't have enough room to transform back into a human. And she didn't have the practical ability to unravel magical chains.

Why had she come here? She knew to steer clear of the market after dark.

Sabine prided herself on being a witch of exceeding practicality. Although she had never, not once, shown any evidence of this trait, she could still feel it brimming under the surface, under the chaos and curiosity. She knew to stay away, to stick to the streets outside bars where drunken humans forgot to be wary of things in the shadows.

But tonight, she sought out the feel of static racing across the hairs, tipping her ears. Longing to breathe in the feral power. Let it surge through her fox form to trail behind her from the tip of her tail, leaving embers of magic in her wake.

Croooaaa sounded far above. The night sky was empty but for stars and a full moon. After a shadow streaked across the latter, Sabine traced its path as it blotted out stars in a widening circle. It flared pitch-black wings before landing on one of the iron brackets supporting the canopy. A scruffy crow bobbed its head at her and croaked again.

"What do you want, you bloated buzzard? Aren't crows supposed to roost at night?" Of course, this was no ordinary crow, and she knew it. And it knew she knew it.

It knew her a little too well, which made its appearance tonight all the more irritating.

In answer, the crow hopped along the bracket, then took a diving plunge straight at her face. Sabine flinched but forced her hands to remain at her sides. She would not defend herself from the decrepit old feather duster. It pulled up at the last moment and landed on her shoulder, where it promptly began picking through her auburn hair.

"Ouch."

Feeling a little louse-y tonight? It asked the question directly into her ear, the tip of its beak pricking her helix piercing. It cawed in laughter at its own pitiful joke and re-situated its talons to get a better grip on the leather strap of her satchel. The strap shifted down her shoulder, and Sabine jerked it back up, unbalancing the feathered menace. Its wings beat frantically at her head as it regained it.

The crow, large for its kind, had most likely been her aunt's familiar, although it denied any such status. Apparently, the death of a Domingue witch threw their familiar into a bit of a tailspin afterwards, or at least it had this one. It had remained in New Orleans, searching for her murderer. Its lice infested fowl had led Sabine to the councilman's dead body and, consequently, to Thibodeaux.

She wasn't sure if she should be thankful or resentful. So, she settled on cursing it as usual and flicking it off her shoulder. It fluttered up and back down.

Not the Faerie Market, it warned her between piercing caws.

"Why not?" she asked, even though she had just enumerated all the reasons to herself before its arrival.

Your rudimentary understanding of magic is no match for the market.

"I wouldn't say rudimentary."

You're just irritable and bored. Getting trapped by a goblin is no cure for boredom. Well . . . It preened its wing feathers. *It will cure the boredom, but you won't like the results. I can't save you from every folly you fall into.*

Sabine wriggled her shoulder, which did nothing to dislodge the beast. "I'm not bored."

Ah. It bobbed its head. *Lonely and reckless, then. I thought finding the scowling man would have cured that.*

"Have you been following me?"

It didn't respond. Instead, it twisted its head to observe the flickering lights of the Faerie Market coming to life and muttered unintelligibly to itself.

"You need to find another witch to pester. I'm not in the market for a familiar."

Craunk.

"Fine, not a familiar. I'm not in need of a companion either. Go eat slugs." Sabine batted it off her shoulder. It croaked curses and flew off, making a dark streak across the stars before disappearing into the night.

Immediately, Sabine felt a wave of loneliness, but she shrugged it off.

She was not bored. Or reckless. Just irritated.

How dare that burly brute of a man throw her out of an obviously magic tainted scene? Well, obvious to her. Of course. Who knew what that lumbering idiot might sense? Which was exactly why he should have begged for her help.

But no, he had that odious woman pat her down and throw her out.

Served him right if the whole affair gobbled him up.

Booths blossomed down aisles before her, like a garden waking to a sunny morning after the rain. Here at the edges of the market were the most dazzling vendors to draw you in. False gold and enchanted silver jewelry encrusted with stones that shone with their own light. Creatures with fanciful plumage squawked from perches. Batik scarves fluttered in the breeze off the river. Brilliant rugs woven with intricate spells flowed off of overburdened tables.

"What harm could come from these?" An ignorant question. But even Sabine, more human than creature, mostly, felt the allure and missed the danger.

The dark heartbeat of the market lay at its center, where patrons wandered in and often failed to return. Sabine knew enough to skirt the dark interior no matter how it tugged at her. The sconces lit with faelight threw a dozen Sabine-shaped shadows in an array around her. As she came closer to that center, the shadows all rotated to point inward, like a compass that had finally caught true north.

Even on the outskirts, she could feel the subtle tug of shadows trying to pull her toward it. Sabine attempted to push her magic against it, knowing it was too meager to fight the market's magic. What she didn't suspect was the market to latch on to her power and drag her in.

Fear caused her to drop her end of the connection.

"Fine. I'm outmatched," she admitted to the market.

The Faerie Market was not the place to practice.

It took a couple of minutes for her heart to slow and her knees to stop shaking. She turned her back to the dark heart of the market and approached a jewel merchant's table. The shiny objects drew her eyes, and her fingers tingled. She didn't need magic to sample the wares.

The gnarled goblin had a pointed chin beneath a cunning smile as he preyed upon two young human women. How did humans get into the Faerie Market?

She suspected the goblin merchant of foul play. He knew not to tempt humans unless they insisted on stumbling into the market on their own, despite the wards. Maybe these two had. Although, they didn't look the type.

The conniving goblin showed the women enchanted trinkets. Sabine didn't have enough experience to decipher the spells, but the subtle buzz floating off the wire tree used to display his wares told her the magic hummed. Not powerful, but insidious. Perhaps she should save these women from whatever game he chose to play. Or maybe she should just screw him over.

"Take your friend and walk away," she whispered in the shorter woman's ear. The woman nodded, looking forlornly at the earrings the goblin had refused to sell her. Sabine retrieved them, attached the faelight earrings to the woman's ears, and rearranged locks of her hair to cover them. "He's not dealing in jewelry. He's dealing in mischief."

Sabine distracted the wretched creature by reorganizing his collection, giving the women the chance to leave. Hopefully, the faelight would reveal enough of the market's true nature to keep them wary.

A treacherous part of her considered liberating a faelight tie pin or cuff links for the detective. He needed something to help him see what went on right under his nose. Not that he would wear them. She sighed and dismissed the idea. Instead, she snagged an audacious jeweled collar meant to tame someone into docilely following all your wishes like an animated doll. Appalling.

This was enough to snag the goblin's attention. He squawked, deserted the two women, and came after Sabine. She threw the necklace over her shoulder to the little beast. Leave while he's distracted, she thought at the women.

But she didn't stick around to see if they did. A minotaur guard had heard the goblin squawking. He bulled his way through the crowd toward her.

Chapter 7

MEGAN

The lights dazzled Meg's vision even after leaving the marketplace as if a filter had been removed between her and the true brilliance of New Orleans. She squinted against the glare. Valdi strolled beside her with a wry smile as if amused by this pedestrian tour of the Big Easy. Although, the violet glow behind her curls told Meg that her roommate was more enchanted by the city than she was willing to let on.

On their way to Bourbon Street, a couple tumbled out of Pat O'Brien's and into Meg, knocking her into the street. She shrieked at an oncoming car before realizing it moved so slowly, due to pedestrians clogging the street, that she was in no danger. Unless *she* decided to charge *it*.

They reached Bourbon, the most famous party street in New Orleans, in the U.S., maybe. But it didn't feel as carefree and decadent as Meg remembered. Well, it did feel decadent, but instead of easygoing, a menacing undercurrent flowed down the street.

Neon sparked against the wavy glass of aged buildings, casting colored light over the crowds on the sidewalks. The air smelled of jazz and spice and the unknown. The people lurching into and out of bars seemed even more peculiar, even for this already peculiar city.

Among the boisterous tourists were a few who moved at a measured pace, eyes roaming, predatory. One of these, an angular man with a feral grin, wove through the crowd toward them. His eyes lit by flames within. His pointed ears perked as if he could hear Meg's breath hitch. The air in front of him was so charged with unsettling energy it made her lungs ache to breathe it in.

"Let's move over a street," she said.

Valdi studied the people streaming into a club as if they were migratory animals. "I thought Bourbon Street was the place to party?"

"Bourbon's for tourists. Royal's where the locals hang out."

"We're local as of 2:00 this afternoon. So, Royal, it is."

This put a glow on Meg. Now she could show her knowledge of the place without the weird vibe of the marketplace or Bourbon. But before Meg could steer her down a side street, Valdi locked eyes with the angular man leering at her. Instead of recoiling, she leaned in, ever curious.

"You can't examine every oddity, Valdi." Meg jerked her aside as the man passed. Valdi let herself be dragged along, but kept her gaze plastered to the strange man.

One block over, Royal made a valiant effort to live up to its name. Buildings stood like stately gentlemen or elegant old dames. Most had dark eyes, watching the more sedate pedestrians pass, cupping hands to look into closed shop windows. Polished antiques crowded up against the other side of the glass, hoping to be admired.

"Are there bars on this street?" Valdi asked.

"Yeah, they're just more spread out." Meg hoped she was right. "Look, there's one. I think."

A block ahead, lights flickered on and off out of a two-story building. As if the whole structure were lit by one neon sign that couldn't decide whether to stay on or not. When the lights flickered off, the building appeared abandoned, shutters closed, doors boarded over. When it flickered on, music blared from open French doors. People danced and shouted within. Then the lights were out, and it appeared abandoned once more.

"Is that some strange projection?" Valdi asked, seeming impressed. "Like a haunted house? Or a ghost building?"

Meg didn't know, but didn't want to admit it. She was busy trying to hide how much the effect unnerved her, sending shivers down her skin even in the warm, humid evening. "Maybe Bourbon Street is not such a bad idea."

"Not a chance. We're here now. I want to know what is going on up there." Valdi picked up pace, and Meg jogged to keep up despite her longer legs. Valdi was on the scent of a puzzle and wouldn't let up until she'd solved it.

As they got closer, the lights held steady. Over the quarter entrance was a neon sign that read Midnight Jazz Club. A couple that Meg hadn't noticed before jostled her as they passed on the sidewalk and headed into the bar. Valdi caught the door before it swung shut and shot a mischievous grin over her shoulder at Meg.

"Coming?"

Inside, the bar didn't have the normal odor of sweaty bodies and spilled liquor that Meg associated with the club scene. Instead, the scent of mint and deep forests hung in the air. The room had that same charged feeling she'd felt since leaving the market. But it had grown more intense.

Apparently, New Orleans had changed quite a bit since she'd last been here. Maybe some New Age movement had cleaned up the old and sultry buildings that she remembered. The clientele certainly weren't tourists in tank tops and worn jeans. But they also weren't locals, either. Everyone moved with a bizarre, fluid grace, as if she were in a room full of ballet dancers. Their long limbs were slightly too slim, slightly too long, slightly too angular to be comfortable to look at.

"Maybe it's a vegan bar?" Meg said out loud without meaning to.

"I don't think so," Valdi said. "But there's definitely something different about them."

As if the whole room had heard them muttering to each other, heads turned to stare. The music from the jazz band ceased, and the room grew unnaturally quiet, like a plug had been pulled on the sound. The band froze, instruments lowered. Mouths parted as if caught in the act of taking their next breath.

The patrons stood unnaturally still. Eyes predatory. Smiles feral.

Chapter 8

<hr>

THIBODEAUX

Screams cut scores down the inside of Jean-Luc's throat. Clawed fingers dragged the breath from him, caving his chest into a hollow. He fell to his knees, one hand grasping at his chest and another at his throat. The edges of his vision pulsed purple, then black, as if the air were bruising before his eyes.

Then the tension holding him upright gave, and he fell forward, his temple catching the edge of a wooden table on the way to the floor. The grasping claws released his breath, and he gasped. His chest filled painfully as he gulped air. Blood painted half his vision in a veil of red. He rolled onto his back, and the room spun drunkenly around him.

His first instinct was to blink his vision clear, but his eyes closed and didn't open until a siren passing outside startled him back to consciousness. Jean-Luc concentrated on the muffled sound of the siren.

Were they coming to assist? Had Carmichael come back and found he'd been attacked?

Rolling onto his side, he pushed himself into a sitting position, waited for the room to settle, and wiped the blood from his brow. It had dried into a thick crust which began bleeding again. He dug a handkerchief from his pocket and put pressure on the wound while surveying the room for his attacker.

The siren moved on, leaving the room in a dull silence. No sound even from the streets below. No movement within.

He pushed himself up cautiously, monitoring for danger.

The apartment was unusually dark for a second story this close to downtown. There should be streetlights. And it was a full moon. A heavy black fog swirled sluggishly through the upper half of the apartment, swallowing any light that attempted to break in through the windows.

Jean-Luc stumbled to the light switch and flipped the overhead on. It must have worked. A yellow glow ignited above the haze, but it did nothing to light the lower half of the room.

His attacker must be in the bedroom if they hadn't left. In no shape to defend himself, Jean-Luc backed toward the open door to the corridor. He wrapped a hand around the frame to support himself as he scanned the hallway, but a membrane across the opening repelled him.

He shoved a shoulder against it until claws broke free and snatched for his breath. And he was screaming up blood once again.

Chapter 9

MEGAN

The Midnight Jazz Club on Royal Street, the club that both was and wasn't there, whose patrons were in full motion or frozen statues, intrigued and terrified Meg. The perfect stillness meant even the slight movement behind the bar startled her. She flinched, and Valdi caught at her arm.

"Is there something I can do for you?" The bartender, a young woman with a fabulous aura of curly hair and a warm brown complexion, cocked her head in their direction. Her brow furrowed as she picked up a glass and wiped it in a contemplative, practiced gesture. Her movements were slow and deliberate, but not abnormally so like the rest of the room.

An older Creole man with a pleasantly creased face dusted with salt and pepper stubble stood just behind her. His hand was at the ready when she passed the dried glass to him. Meg was sure his hands had been at his side a moment before. When had he moved?

"We're just clubbing," Valdi said with confidence. Her eyes studied the figures closest to them with the intensity of an archaeologist examining a herd of animals inexplicably trapped in amber.

In front of them was a man with improbably wide shoulders and green eyes. He alone looked out of place among the willowy crowd. His eyes narrowed as if confused to find them in his path.

Meg started to excuse herself for being in his way when the room broke loose, filling the space with the sound of heels striking hardwood, clothes brushing against skin, and the audible sound of the saxophone player taking that breath at last.

Swallowing the lump of beignet that had risen into her throat, Meg asked, "Is this a private club?"

The bartender casually glanced around the room, sighed, and said, "You're welcome, I guess. Come on in," right before the music blasted back through the space in a wave that Meg could feel as it hit her chest.

She took a step back, ready to leave, but Valdi dove into the crowd, her head bobbing at least a foot below everyone else. Meg tried to track her, but she disappeared into the mass of people swaying on the dance floor. The bartender shook her head as if disappointed in a negligent child, then gave Meg a half smile before the crowd hid her from view.

Meg dove in after Valdi. Dancers undulated around her. Each moved separately, caught up in their own dance, but the mass of them moved with a single rhythm.

Their bodies parted almost imperceptibly, allowing her to pass and closing behind her. It felt like she was a lamb being herded into a trap. If it weren't for Valdi, Meg would've backed out before the wolves turned to find her in their midst.

A tawny man with a beak-ish nose and thick circular glasses watched her progress from a table near the open French doors. Watching the man, Meg nearly bumped into Valdi. She had ventured so far into the crowd that she found herself emerging from the other side.

Valdi approached an odd couple on the far wall. A voluptuous female with an enormous, textured bag hanging from her shoulder by a slim silver chain stood next to an androgynous person with a bizarrely slim mustache.

The left arm of the mustache appeared to curl upward, moving on its own to beckon them. Valdi accepted this unspoken invitation.

"How odd," she said, voice raised to be heard over the jazz band to their right. "It appears as if your mustache is moving of its own accord."

"I assure you, me and my mustache are both in agreement. Good of you to join us." The sides of the mustache curled and uncurled in a cartoonish mega-villain manner.

"You are an odd little creature to be here. And you," The voluptuous woman with green hair that flowed over her shoulders like kelp studied Meg. "You're her pet, I presume. Does Zula know you are here?" The woman kept her arm wrapped protectively around her bag, as if she suspected Valdi and Meg intended to steal it. The pair smelled faintly of fish and oil slicks.

"Zula?" Valdi asked. "We don't know anyone here at the bar. Or in New Orleans, really."

"You're certainly not in New Orleans here, love," the mustached person said. "You are in the In Between. And Zula de Bonaire is the owner of the Midnight Jazz Club."

"It's a Fae only bar," the woman said, looking first at Valdi, then Meg up and down as if she were deciding whether it was worth her effort to have the two of them thrown out. Apparently deciding not, she looked off into the crowd, dismissing their presence.

Meanwhile, the odd mustaches continued to writhe above pursed lips. It didn't appear to be composed of individual hairs, but rather each side seemed to be a solid whip like appendage.

Valdi reached to touch one.

"Don't," Meg squeaked, but the whisker had already wrapped around Valdi's pointer finger. It drew the finger to those pursed lips for a delicate kiss. Meg realized she was gaping and snapped her mouth shut.

"They're like the whiskers on a catfish," Valdi said, seeming way too excited at seeing live mustaches.

"Exactly like, one might say." The pursed lips spread out into a wide smile, a little too wide.

"Percival, don't toy with the human. You are so tiresome," the woman said.

Meg tugged at her roommate, attempting to remove them from the couple and the bar without drawing too much attention, if possible. But Valdi resisted.

Apparently determined to ingratiate herself with these people, she complimented the woman's hideous bag. "Your snake skin purse is extraordinary. I assume from the uninterrupted pattern that it's synthetic, or from an anaconda."

The woman with kelp hair turned a withering look on her.

"Alligator," she said.

"Oh, wow. They allow alligator farming down here? Or do you trap them?" Valdi asked, reaching for the bag. To Meg's horror, she stroked the side of the bag without asking for permission. A stubby snout attached to the bag swung around from under the woman's arm and snapped pointed teeth at her. Instead of jumping back, Valdi leaned in.

Meg screeched.

Valdi laughed.

The mustached mouth smirked.

"Do you often paw other creatures without their permission?" the woman asked, tucking the bag up against her chest as its head curled back into her side.

"They're tourists, Cassandra. Don't be so prickly. And keep Leonard in check. He shouldn't be so touchy if he wants to come out with us."

"She grabbed at him," the woman insisted, hugging the bag protectively.

Meg prickled at the accusation. "We're not tourists. We live here."

Valdi spoke over her. "I apologize for being so rude. We are new to the area, but that's no excuse. I know to keep my hands to myself."

The mustached mouth smiled that too wide smile, and the woman flipped the kelp hair behind her shoulder, making a begrudging expression of tolerance. "At least you can admit you're wrong. Most humans are clueless."

"Cass, don't be so judgmental."

Cass's face screwed up, but Valdi jumped in. "No, no. Cassandra's right. Us simple, uhm, humans can't be trusted to recognize our own rudeness."

The woman shrugged off the apology and left. Her companion bowed first to Valdi, taking her hand and kissing her knuckles, then did the same to Meg before following.

Valdi headed in the opposite direction, obviously intent on accosting another of the strange clientele. Meg attempted to follow her, but a tall man stepped into her path.

Surprisingly, the man had several inches on her, most didn't. His skin was so pale that it was almost blue, and his hair shone like moonlight, brushing his shoulders. His icy eyes had snagged on the charmless charm bracelet. His ice-blue gaze nipped her wrist like the beginning of frostbite. A chill worked its way up her arm as the man's eyes tracked from her bracelet, up her arm, across her clavicle, over her neck, and came to her eyes.

The corner of his mouth hitched, revealing a line of bright, sharp teeth. Startled, Meg blinked, then realized it was really only a sultry smile of invitation. He offered his hand to her, long, slim fingers gracefully held out, steady and waiting.

His cool grip closed tight on hers. Meg tried to remember taking his hand as he swept her onto the dance floor. The cool man twirled her around to land in the circle of his arms.

Jazz engulfed her senses, removing the other dancers from her peripheral vision, leaving only this enigmatic man. His icy eyes pricked her senses, and Meg felt all her thoughts and memories must be laid bare to this oddly beautiful stranger. He pulled her close, pressing his lips against the curve of her ear. She felt his teeth graze her skin, and warmth trickled down the length of her throat.

Attempting to laugh off the sensation, Meg spoke loud enough that she might be heard over the music. "You're not a vampire, are you?"

His laugh brushed her cheek and sent a chill winding down her spine. If he hadn't kept a tight grip around her waist, she feared her knees might've collapsed. But he spun her lightly across the floor as if they didn't require solid ground beneath their feet.

When he spoke, the movement of his jaw set a silver crescent moon swinging from his earlobe. "No vampires allowed in The Midnight Jazz Club. You'll have to go to another bar for that sort of entertainment. Is that what you want?"

This last question was spoken directly into her ear, setting ablaze every inch of her that had been chilled only a moment before.

"No," she said, breathless. Embarrassed by her reaction, she pulled away, but he did not let her go. He just looked down at her and smiled.

This time, she was not mistaken at the sharpness of his teeth.

Chapter 10

✦━━━━━━━━━✦

SABINE

The air grew thick in anticipation of a storm brewing over the Gulf. The crisp breeze of a few hours earlier had grown heavy and surly, which suited Sabine's mood. The odor d'tourist stung her human nose. If she shifted to her fox form, the smells would be more intriguing, telling her who ate where, which musician played in which bar, and who'd made out with whom in which alley. It became a game, but relieving tourists of their poorly guarded goods was simpler in human form.

She swayed in and around the flow of tourists seeking the next best bar in their desperate search for the magic of New Orleans. They didn't know that it stayed clear of Bourbon Street, where the city performed a sleight of hand to entertain the visitors. It hid its real magic in the Tremé, in the crevices of the city's cemeteries not trafficked by walking and buggy tours, and the edges that brushed up against a bayou swallowed in the dark beyond the city lights.

Sabine performed her own sleight of hand along Bourbon, saving her meager magic for the shadowy alleys, the In Between spaces. On Bourbon, outside Pat O'Brien's, she allowed drunken men and women to stumble into her as they tried to orient themselves toward their hotel or an Uber. She'd gently righted them on their wobbly legs while removing the inconvenient weight of their wallets, their purses, their phones, their jewelry.

The crystal earrings, silver chains, and gold rings were not as easily transformed into money for life-sustaining food and lattes, but Sabine had an eye for sparkly things. You would think that her first, and only, animal form would have been a magpie rather than a fox. She had a lovely collection of trinkets in the nest she'd built on the upper floor of an abandoned townhouse.

Her aunt's murder had sent Sabine into hiding the very same day, and she'd never quite gotten out of the habit of living in the shadows. Only the detective and the mite ridden crow knew of the nest she'd built for herself in the old building. And she trusted them, or him, anyway.

The crow was still a big question mark.

Sabine rarely wore any of the jewelry. Not that she feared being caught. The police only had so much time to hunt for lost baubles when they had more nefarious crimes to deal with. But she would bring out the shiny treasures and line them along her windowsill. There, high above the street, the moonlight infused them with its magic.

With her satchel loaded, Sabine left Bourbon Street and made her way to the quieter Royal Street. Walking among the closed antique shops and shuttered homes, she felt the oddly comforting sensation that she was a wraith. Unseen. Lost in time.

Ahead, a faint glimmer gave away the glamour laid over a shuttered building. Sabine wondered if she'd had the chance to train with her aunt, if she would be able to see the shape of the glamour or what hid beneath it.

The zing of enchantment against her skin as she traveled the streets of New Orleans told her that real magic hid just out of sight. The Faerie Market only appeared when the vendors wished to toy with humans. Like that squat goblin trying to palm off cursed trinkets on those two women. What game had he been playing at?

As she contemplated the two clueless women, magic flared purple and gold from the glamour. As if bidden by Sabine's thoughts, one of the women stumbled onto the street, breathless and dazed. The taller one who'd been trying to impress her friend with her limited knowledge of the Big Easy.

The woman looked about her as if she'd lost something or someone. After a moment, she seemed to orient herself and headed toward the residential area.

Curious, Sabine followed.

The woman disappeared in the shadows between streetlights, but the charmed bracelet on her wrist flickered with magic.

Sabine told herself that she followed to be sure the dazed woman made it unmolested to her destination. But Sabine knew when she was lying to herself, mostly. It was the bracelet that she pursued.

Shiny and enchanted.

How could she resist?

They wove down alleys, across streets, circling back more than once before the young woman got her bearings and began walking with a purpose. She paused at the side door of a cottage. After several minutes of searching her purse for keys—in which time, Sabine considered finding them for her—she let herself in, forgetting to lock it behind her.

Not that it mattered, Sabine had taught herself the trick of picking these old tumbler locks. An unlocked door lacked the excitement of a challenge.

Sabine slipped into her fox form and jumped the fence to the tiny backyard, where she climbed up a drooping oak. Perched on a branch, she waited. The woman's silhouette eventually appeared behind the glass of a second-story window without turning on the lights. Just as Sabine had guessed, two women, new to town on limited income, crammed together in a second-story apartment.

With her fox ears, Sabine could hear the woman muttering to what must be her roommate, apologizing for coming in late. Then, admonishing that same roommate for leaving her alone in downtown. Her companion didn't seem to feel the need to respond. Most likely passed out.

One of the windows opened, and the woman asked her silent roommate, "Does it smell in here to you? Did you throw up? I'm not cleaning up."

A few more stumbled steps, then springs creaked as the woman apparently put herself to bed. In under a minute, a nasally, drunken snore told Sabine she was good to go.

With the open window, she wouldn't even need to bother with the unlocked door. It just got easier and easier to prey upon these simple souls. Tomorrow, they might tell themselves a sneak thief had let themselves in that way, before finding their door unlocked.

Sabine scaled the tree and navigated across an obliging limb. She nimbly jumped from it to the windowsill. Her nose twitched. There was definitely an unpleasant organic smell. She shifted back into human form to escape the nuances of it.

If it was vomit, she didn't need to know the particular composition.

A vanity mirror doubled the enchanted glow of the bracelet. Sabine left it in place and made a circuit of the apartment. A short, round figure lay on the couch with one arm hanging over the side. She no longer wore the enchanted amethyst earrings that Sabine had graciously gifted her at the goblin vendor's expense.

A quick search of the living room revealed nothing. She crept up to the couch to see if the woman had them in her hand, but she slipped in something viscous on the floor.

"Ew." The thought of vomit on her slippers decided for Sabine that she could live without the earrings. There was no glow giving them away. She'd probably lost them, or they'd been stolen by someone who knew their real worth.

Back in the bedroom, Sabine picked up the chain from the vanity. Delicate charms dangled from the gold chain. A silver crescent moon. A stone wolf with an amber eye. An enamel owl whose head turned to observe her.

The creak of the mattress proceeded a confused voice spoke behind her.

"Valdi?"

Sabine dropped into fox form, snatched up the bracelet in her teeth, and jumped out the window, then to the tree. She'd scampered down the trunk and out onto the street, before noticing that she tracked bloody paw prints behind her.

Chapter 11

MEGAN

"Valdi, are you awake?" Meg asked from the narrow twin bed under one side of the sloping ceiling.

The daylight cut through the sheer curtains to hook Meg's eyelids like barbs. The pillowcase stuck to her cheek, glued with drool. Her leg muscles had frozen into knots of wood from a night of dancing. The balls of her feet pulsed with newly hatched blisters.

Groaning in the universal language of the damned, she rolled onto her side and cracked an eye to check the twin bed on the opposite wall, lit by the agonizing fire of the first morning light.

Valdi hadn't made it to the room. Oh, yeah. She'd dropped on the couch after leaving Meg at the bar on her own. She was not surprised Valdi remembered her way back. She was a walking GPS tracker, unlike Meg, who barely found her way in the dark. She would have used the navigation on her phone, but it gave out once she walked into the bar and hadn't started even after leaving.

If it had, maybe Meg could've checked the time. And maybe not spent all night in one bar. Maybe she wouldn't be a wreck this morning.

She wondered how Valdi was doing, then remembered the smell. She was probably fine after being sick. Valdi believed she was so clever, but she couldn't hold her liquor.

A wave of resentment tried to rear its head in Meg's gut, but nausea overtook it. She sprinted to the bathroom and very nearly made it to the toilet before her stomach revolted. A rainbow of mixed drinks painted the side of the white porcelain. With the floor drenched, Meg had nowhere to kneel, so she slouched against the wall with her head over the bowl.

Her stomach emptied but continued to dry heave for several minutes in an attempt to be thorough.

Afterwards, she gingerly stepped over the puddle of despair on the floor and turned the sink's antique hot and cold knobs, round and round, until the water begrudgingly agreed to dribble out. She flushed her mouth. She washed her face. She brushed her teeth, then bravely examined her reflection in the mottled mirror.

"Ew." How did vomit end up in her ear?

She scrubbed it out while feeling unreasonably certain that this was somehow Valdi's fault for abandoning her. If she had tapped Meg to tell her she was leaving, Meg would've followed. She was sure of it.

Meg squinted at her reflection and struggled to remember. Maybe Valdi had told her? She'd said something about leaving. Meg dredged through the murky memories of the night before, trying to find evidence for or against her roommate, but failed.

"Valdi! Wake up. I'm not cleaning up if you lost your shit all over the carpet out there," Meg announced as she mopped up her own mess off the white hexagon tiles, leaving revolting red stains in the grout. She'd scrub it out later.

It took both hand towels, a washcloth, and a bath towel to sop it all up. She dumped them in the tub and ran the shower over the whole mess in hopes it would magically disappear down the drain while she checked on Valdi.

It was no wonder Valdi couldn't hold her liquor. She'd never been to New Orleans before. It took a while to become a true local, knowing when to call it quits. Meg would have to show her.

Unwilling to address the mess on the carpet, Meg took the long route behind the couch to the abbreviated galley kitchen. Her wobbly thoughts needed caffeine, but her resentful stomach demanded something soft and solid to sop up the remaining acid first.

"I'm making toast. You want some?" Still no answer. "Fine. Sleep it off."

There was only one slice of sourdough left, anyway. She set the toaster, then her stomach roiled, and she popped up the bread untoasted and scarfed it down while searching the drawer for a French vanilla coffee pod.

Valdi tried to come across as a solid, reasonable person, but she was fragile under her geared exterior. She'd need to toughen up here.

With her forehead against the upper cabinet, Meg inhaled the vanilla coffee flavored steam. She stuffed the rest of the stale bread into her mouth and screwed her eyes shut. When they'd moved in, she'd wished the kitchen had a window, but this morning, she was grateful it didn't.

The day hadn't fully started, and she could barely stand it. With her head against the cabinet, she took the first scalding sip of coffee, then pushed herself upright and carried it into the living room to assess the damage.

Leaning over the back of the couch, Meg prodded Valdi's shoulder. But her roommate was out so cold that she didn't grunt or squirm or react at all. After another swallow, Meg felt marginally better.

She whispered in Valdi's ear. "Wake up sleepy head."

Nothing.

"I'm not cleaning that up." Meg pointed to the carpet with her mug.

The rag rug was soaked. The white fibers were stained the same blood red of the grout in the bathroom. But at the edges, instead of the brilliant color of strawberry margarita it had turned the rust color of dried blood.

Meg jerked as she recognized it for what it was. Coffee spilled down Valdi's arm, but she did not move. Did not make a noise. Did not react at all.

"Valdi?"

"Valdi!"

Chapter 12

✦

SABINE

The sky blushed from its memory of the past night. Tourists and locals squinted at the arrival of a new dawn. Some pulled the blinds and plunged back under covers to relive the evening in their dreams. Others to recover from it. A few stretched and yawned and greeted the sun, thanking it for a chance to start over.

Sabine was among the latter. She woke with the city to prowl the streets. In fox form, she slipped out of the loose grate on the ground floor of her abandoned townhouse.

Although she and the detective had discovered who was responsible for her aunt's death, Sabine didn't trust staying in the house where she'd been murdered. She didn't know what would become of it. Back in her human form, she made her regular circuit past the home.

The house looked as if it slept, waiting to be gently shaken awake. Except for the dried ferns slumped over the edges of their hanging pots. And a bullet hole in the kitchen cabinet. And the bloodstain on the linoleum floor.

Sabine jangled the newly acquired charm bracelet around her wrist in an effort to clear her mind of the gruesome scene. As if summoned by the jingling of the charms, a crow-shaped shadow crossed her path, followed by a harsh *Craaw, Craaw*.

Sabine refused to look up. That carrion crow was the lonely one, not her. She might feel sorry for him, left behind when the Domingue witch died, if he weren't such a pest. He was not the only one abandoned. Sabine didn't wail about being left to her own devices in a city she barely knew with magic she scarcely understood.

She made do on her own.

Last night, she'd been mostly business minded, collecting wallets, cash, cards. Until she'd met the detective, and he'd handled her like a common criminal. She was anything but common, and he should know it. His foul attitude was to blame for her detour into the Faerie Market. And the dark region at the center that she was not equipped to handle.

Wings beat at the side of her head as the crow landed on her shoulder. Sabine closed her eyes against the onslaught and kept walking beneath the tree lined sidewalk as the creature settled itself, talons digging into the leather strap of her satchel.

Dangling the crime in front of the detective. The crow bobbed its head, its beak slicing close to Sabine's cheek. *Excellent strategy to capture his attention.*

Sabine swatted at him. He dodged, flapping up, then back down onto her shoulder, where he began to preen her hair, pulling strands loose from her ponytail.

"Don't you have a garbage heap to inspect?"

In answer to her comment, the crow rolled his head from side to side as if searching for a worthy trashcan. Stupid animal. He was definitely wrong about her seeking the detective's attention. Thibodeaux was too suspicious for his own good, or for hers.

The charms hanging from the bracelet tickled her palm. Sabine had only been helping two unsuspecting humans escape the market, then the one woman tripped back into Sabine's path later in the evening. It was clearly fate asking Sabine to relieve the clueless woman of the enchanted jewelry.

"Too dangerous for a human to be walking around New Orleans with a gift from a goblin," she told the crow.

Craunk.

"What do you know? I'm not human. Well, I am, but I'm more."

Or I could be if I had someone to teach me.

Sabine dangled the gold chain in front of the bird. "Where did that woman get all these charms? I only saw an empty chain bracelet at the market in the middle of all that clutter."

The crow just muttered and went back to preen her until a good third of her hair hung loose from its tie.

As she dropped her hand, she noticed a dark crescent of dried blood stubbornly remained under one of her nails. It collected there when she'd fallen into fox form. What had happened in that apartment? The pungent smell still coated her nostrils. How had she not recognized it immediately? She'd just assumed. Making assumptions had never served her well before. Why should it now?

Craaw. Craaw.

"It's not my blood. It was in the apartment of one of those women we saw at the Faerie Market. They left with this bracelet, minus the charms, and a pair of faelight earrings. That must be how they found their way into that bar. It was warded. It must exist in the In Between. Then they come home with a bracelet filled with charms and blood on the floor." Sabine twisted her head to look at the crow. "Does that sound like a coincidence to you?"

Creeek.

"I know. Nothing about the Fae is ever a coincidence."

The crow muttered.

"No, I didn't stay around to find out. I was busy, saving her from this." She jangled the bracelet, and it sparked against her skin like static electricity. "Why did the market open to them? And why did that goblin let a human leave with this?"

Mutter.

"Nothing is free at the Faerie Market. And it might have cost one of them their life."

Mutter.

"I don't know about the other. Do you think I should go see if she's okay?"

Silence proceeded a hard tug, and the crow turned its head with strands of auburn hair dangling from its beak.

"Ow! I'm trying to talk business here." She snatched her hair out of its beak and stuffed it into a side pocket on her satchel. It wasn't wise to leave stray hairs around the city. Especially not with a once-familiar to a once-powerful witch.

"You lived with Nanny. Surely, you picked up something. What do they do?" Sabine shook the charms in front of the crow. It attempted to catch one. "Nope, they're mine. I stole them fair and square with no help from you."

Another tug, but Sabine's hair stayed stubbornly rooted.

"Cut it out or I'll stuff and roast you."

Craunk.

"Whatever. So, if there's a body, they'll probably call in the detective, right?"

Mutter.

"I am not interested in seeing that surly man. But he will need my help if someone was hurt using magic. He is hopelessly blind to it."

Craaw, Craaw.

"I am not blind to it. I know it's there. I just don't know exactly what to do with it. And I can't really see it."

Mutter.

"It *is* different." Sabine cut through the St. Louis Cemetery, not too far from the women's apartment. If any ghosts approached, she could always ask if they'd seen a newcomer. But none did.

If ghosts existed, Sabine had never seen one. She walked the rows of concrete crypts built as homes to the dead. Right after her aunt's death, she'd frequented the Greenwood Cemetery near her aunt's house in hopes that her aunt might meet her there.

She never did.

"Thibodeaux'll be grumpy. Murders get under his skin. He's too softhearted. He tries to hide it, but I can tell."

A shadow ducked behind one of the crypts. Sabine hesitated, considering if she should check for a wraith. But it might just be a junky sleeping off a bad night. Better leave them alone, corporeal or not.

She resumed her monologue. "He'll try to keep me out, assuming I'm just as delicate as he is."

Afraid you'll take something, the crow said.

Sabine shrugged. "He'll want to talk to me. I'm kind of a witness. I saw them at the market, then again stumbling out of the bar."

Creeek.

"No, I won't tell him I went inside."

Mutter.

"He won't see the paw prints. He's not that observant."

Mutter.

"Maybe you're right." Sabine took off the charm bracelet and stuffed it into her pouch. "I'll keep quiet and just observe."

Craaw, Craaw.

"I can to be quiet."

Chapter 13

MEGAN

The police had Meg sitting on a bar stool facing the kitchen, but she couldn't help but take darting glances over her shoulder at the tacky blood on the floor. It had spread under the secondhand olive vinyl armchair and out the other side. Her mother had found it on the curb in front of a house in the nearby Abita Springs. Meg planned to paint a splatter design over it once she figured out which paint would stick to vinyl.

Valdi's blood had pooled around the square wooden leg. Would it soak into the wood? How could she get it out? Could she paint over it? Would the paint stick to blood-soaked wood?

"Ms. Armand?" the female officer said.

Had she asked a question?

"Ma'am?"

"Officer Carmichael," the officer said. "Ms. Armand, you were telling me that you and Valdi moved in together yesterday, and you were bar hopping last night to celebrate. Did I get that right?"

"She's going to Tulane, and I was going to get a job. We're splitting the rent." Meg said, reliving the discussion they'd had over sangrias at Babalu in Memphis after traveling to Chicago to meet Valdi's parents. She glanced back at the blood, Valdi's blood. Her chest heaved as a cry fought its way up, but Meg's throat constricted, catching it before it erupted.

Officer Carmichael, who'd been scribbling on a notepad, paused to study Meg's face. "Is there something else you need to tell me?"

Meg tried to control the shock and grief as she spoke. "She *was*—I meant to say, she *was* going to Tulane. We *were* going to split the rent. We had plans. She had plans. I don't know what went wrong." A sob hiccuped out, but she arrested it.

Meg knew what went wrong.

Her friend lay dead. Murdered in their apartment cut out of this century-old cottage near the heart of New Orleans. Someone had come in and stolen her friend's life. If Valdi had come for her—told her she was leaving the bar—they would have come home together.

And both been killed?

But why?

"Did you find anything missing?" the officer asked calmly while her fellow officers poured over the apartment like a kicked anthill.

"I haven't looked. I called you. Should I have looked?"

"No, that's okay. Did anyone come home with you?"

Did they? She felt like she was being followed, but?

"No," Meg said.

"Which clubs did you go to?"

Meg could see a flickering light, then an image of the neon sign emerged. "The Midnight Jazz Club," she said before the memory winked out again.

An officer exchanged a skeptical look with Carmichael. "Where is this Midnight Jazz Club? I haven't heard of it."

"Uhm, on Royal. Yeah, that's where we were."

"Just the one place?"

"Yes."

"Did anyone there make you feel uncomfortable?"

Meg's mind froze. Did they? Her arms broke out into chill bumps. It seemed that someone had unnerved her. But who? She shook her head.

"No disconcerting stranger approaching either you or Valdi, to your knowledge?"

Meg felt her mouth gaping open, and she shut it. Disconcerting. Yes. But she couldn't picture the stranger.

While she fumbled through her memories for an answer, an officer called from the bedroom. "These prints headed into the bedroom are a size five, maybe five and a half."

"What prints?" Meg asked. She hadn't been back in the bedroom since she'd found Valdi on the couch. She'd called the police and positioned herself on the stool where she could watch all the doors and windows and not see the body.

The officer questioning Meg scowled. "Thank you," she said to the one measuring footprints. "I don't suppose you wear a size five?" she asked, looking skeptically at Meg's feet.

Meg shook her head, and the second officer yelled again. "And a size eight smudged the initial prints, headed back into the living room."

Her questioner rolled her eyes, apparently yelling out information wasn't her idea of good police work. When the officer raised her eyebrow, Meg nodded.

Yes, she wore a size eight, and must have smudged the prints on her way out this morning. Realization crept up on her.

"Someone was here after I came home?" Her chest heaved, her breath coming in fits and starts. The woman got off her stool and gently pushed Meg's head between her knees.

"Slow down. You're fine. If someone was here, they didn't want to harm you."

Meg's head popped back up. "But why? Why Valdi? Why not me? Why?"

The hiccuping sobs threatened to take over, and Meg tucked her head back between her knees in hopes of stopping them. Falling apart now wouldn't help. While she practiced remembering how to breathe, the officers discussed whether to move her directly to a hotel. Or whether she should go to the precinct first for further questioning.

It hadn't occurred to her she would have to leave.

It hadn't occurred to her she might have to stay either.

Neither option seemed right.

Her friend was dead. Something bigger should happen. Bigger than her being shuttled from one place to another. Bigger than packing an overnight bag. Shouldn't there be sirens blaring in the streets, bunting down the killer?

"Miss?" the officer said.

"What?" Meg sat up straight, nearly yelling in the woman's face. "Why are you all so calm? What is wrong with you? My friend is right there." Meg jumped off the stool and pointed at the couch.

Her eyes landed on Valdi for the first time since she had called the cops.

And the world stopped.

For a moment, the cops were gone.

The blood disappeared, and it was no longer her friend lying there but a stranger.

A long-limbed, dark-skinned man.

And she started to scream.

And scream.

And scream.

Chapter 14

CARMICHAEL

The limbs swayed and creaked like old bones. Rattled by the sound, Carmichael searched the oak. For what, she didn't know. Maybe the ghost of that poor girl in the body bag.

No ghosts.

Stick to the script, she told herself.

Megan Armand meekly folded herself into the driver's seat of her red, oxidized Buick, and Carmichael shut the door. Megan wrapped her arms around her torso and slumped forward like a rag doll with her head against the steering wheel.

The screen door creaked, and Johnson came out the side door carrying the woman's overnight bag. They'd directed her to pack a couple of changes of clothes and toiletries. Megan had gathered her things while dazed, as if navigating a dream, a bad one.

"Thibodeaux would know how to handle this," Carmichael said to no one in particular. She depended on him more than she'd like to admit. He'd been all over the simple missing person's case yesterday. Now, he was missing himself.

Johnson tapped the window and waved at Megan. Poor woman jumped at the sight of his face right next to the glass. He chuckled and opened the door to deposit her overnight bag on the passenger seat.

Carmichael punched his arm. He shrugged as if he had no clue what he'd done wrong. He probably didn't. Idiot.

"She just lost her shit," he said, loud enough for the woman to hear. Carmichael glared, but he didn't take the hint. "She saw the body, right? Before she called 9-1-1. Maybe it was too dark for her to really see what was going on. But, wow, she lost it."

Carmichael leaned over to check on the woman huddled behind the wheel while giving directions to Johnson. "You follow her. I'll be there after I lock up."

Johnson leaned in close but didn't drop his voice. "You think she did it?"

Carmichael shoved him back. "She's barely holding it together. Don't make it worse."

"She's either faking it, or having delusions. Probably feeling guilty about offing her roommate. Lovers fight, maybe." This time, Johnson caught Carmichael's glare. "What?"

"You can't go jumping to conclusions. Thibodeaux says don't start making up your mind before you've seen all you can see and heard all you can hear."

"He should've been here."

"Yep."

"Where is he? He's always first on the scene."

Carmichael nodded. "Always first to talk to the witness. He hates secondhand info. I called him. I'd never hear the end of it if I didn't. Twice before leaving the office, once on the way, and then before going up."

"He never turns off his phone. I'd've bet he showers with it," Johnson said as he sauntered toward the police cruiser.

"I'd have put my money on that, too." Carmichael's nerves were on edge. Where was the detective? "Last I saw him was yesterday. He went back into Tyler Davis's apartment, that missing man. Said he was checking on something. Told me to go on ahead. He'd walk back."

"Weird. You think he was mugged?"

Carmichael shook her head. "No. Not likely anyone could catch him off guard. He likes to walk when he needs to think."

Johnson rounded the Buick out of earshot, but Carmichael continued as if he were listening. "I'll run by his apartment after work if he doesn't come in. See if he's down with the flu or something."

She remembered Thibodeaux had taken that delinquent pickpocket to his apartment once to keep her safe. Then, he lets her flounce into a crime scene. Carmichael didn't think they were lovers. The snarky little thief irritated him more than anything, as far as Carmichael could tell. But he did seem to think she had insight that the rest of them didn't. Maybe she had more street smarts than Carmichael gave her credit for, but she doubted it.

Car doors slammed in quick succession. The lead cruiser stopped traffic, its lights on but no siren. Another stopped further down the street. The Buick in between stalled as Megan tried to pull away from the curb. She ground the starter before finally maneuvering behind the cruiser.

Carmichael turned back to the gate and noticed blood splatters trailing down the sidewalk. She raised a hand and called out.

"Hold up."

Megan's car lurched to a stop. The cruisers idled, waiting for Carmichael's signal. She motioned for them to roll down the window. Confused, Megan lowered hers, as well, while Carmichael ordered the lab techs back out.

"Take a sample." She tapped beside the spot with the toe of her shoe. "Someone was dripping blood when they left the site."

The tech shook her head, ponytail swaying. "Nope, not splatters. Those are prints."

Carmichael knelt to take a closer look.

The tech crouched beside her. "Pawprints," she clarified. "Looks like a canine, maybe. Except the gate's wrong. Looks more like a—"

"Fox!" Megan shrieked through the open window. The distraught woman stretched across the passenger seat and frantically pointed out the window.

Another delusion, Carmichael thought. Maybe Johnson was right, and Megan Armand was crazed with guilt, or grief. But why a fox? That was the problem. Carmichael couldn't tell. She needed Thibodeaux. The realization was irritating. She should be able to do this herself.

"Down the block. A fox. It came out of the gate," Megan yelled.

Carmichael nodded and waved Megan and the cruisers away as she reluctantly looked in the direction the woman had pointed.

Sure enough, a bushy auburn tail swished behind the haunches of a red fox as it darted down the street and around the corner.

Chapter 15

SABINE

Idiots, all of them. Thibodeaux better thank her for fixing this for him, Sabine thought as she turned the corner.

Where was the detective? He wouldn't have missed her tracks.

If Carmichael was going to check out his apartment and spoon feed him chicken gumbo, Sabine'd have to do the real detective work. Other than maybe Thibodeaux, she was the only one equipped to do any good. Sabine had lost all faith in his officers to figure out what was going on.

No, that wasn't true. She hadn't had faith in them in the first place. Thibodeaux had some sense, true. But he hadn't lent any of it to his crew.

Luckily, if he'd been there, he'd have guessed those were her bloody fox prints on the sidewalk. And he'd have known who they belonged to. That would be difficult to explain. He'd default to blaming her for thieving, of course. As he was wont to do.

Not that she hadn't been thieving, but he shouldn't automatically suspect her. Although it was quite nice of him to think about her so often. Sabine felt a wolfish grin spread across her fox face.

While Carmichael was busy questioning the hysterical roommate. Sabine would be out doing the real work. She was sure that woman was dead due to some magical fuckery. Probably instigated by that gnarled goblin from the market.

Even if Thibodeaux was doing his job, which he obviously wasn't, he was no use when it came to magic.

First stop, the glammed up bar.

Sabine considered running across town in fox form. She could dart in and out of streets with hardly anyone taking notice. If the locals saw her, they wouldn't care. The tourists, as far as they knew, the New Orleans streets could be teeming with wildlife, coming in from the bayou nearby. They probably figured the neighborhoods were crawling with alligators once the sun went down.

The great reptiles might've been a nuisance to the city if they weren't busy sunning themselves during the day and just plain lazy after dark.

But her paws were sore. So Sabine settled back into her human form and caught a streetcar to Bourbon. She got off and walked from there.

The heavily trafficked street cleared as the sun rose, exposing it for the gaudy tourist trap it was. By daylight, it turned from a neon coated strip of mild debauchery to a dingy relic. It patiently waited while the tourists slept through the day, then, when the sun went down, it turned back on.

One street over, the daytime foot traffic was more polished, trading between antique shops and restaurants. Royal stood as the barrier between the bars of Bourbon and parishioners of St. Louis Cathedral. Its cast iron columns were freshly painted.

Brick repointed. Windows clear and sparkling to show off delicately distressed antiques within.

And then came the offending building from the night before, disrupting the reputable streetscape.

The stately old curmudgeon of a building slumped on a corner of Royal Street. Its doors and windows were shuttered and locked against the public. Eaves drooped with despair. Balconies sagged with sorrow. Brick crumbled in defeat.

It all looked a little too derelict to be real. It lacked imagination. A bit of artistry. Maybe it was just that Sabine knew a glamour hid the face of the real building. She wondered if she would have noticed the mirage if she hadn't seen it flicker when Meg tripped out of it the night before.

The familiar crow landed on the rusted balcony railing and made a rather obscene caw at her. She flipped it the bird. "You don't have to tell me. I can see there's a spell on it, you feathered bag-of-bones."

The crow circled her and landed at her feet, picking at a string of plastic beads just to be sure it wasn't something tasty.

"Bird brain, you can't eat that."

A woman with rich brown skin, a fabulous fro, and purple-tinted sunglasses walked down the middle of Royal toward the building. A well-aged Cadillac swerved as they caught sight of her and nearly clipped the side mirror of a parked car. It honked its disapproval. But the woman continued to saunter down the center as if she had no care for the brazen language of vehicles. She moved with a confidence almost as contrived as the building's decorative decay. Both a little too perfectly polished to be true.

Sabine turned her back on the street and observed the woman's reflection in the antique shop window. The fabulous woman hesitated long enough to take in her surroundings. Apparently assured no one watched her, she turned and walked straight through the shutters, barring entry to the derelict building.

"I knew it."

Craunk.

"I said I knew it." Sabine stalked across the street, mid-block to the sound of honking horns.

The crow hopped along behind her, muttering its infernal string of inane questions. "Why're you here? Not your crime? Ahh," which came out as more of a creek, catching Sabine's attention. "It's the detective again. You want to impress him. Very clever. Very. If you knew anything about solving crime."

"I haven't given up on the plan to have you stuffed, you know."

Creeek.

"Then keep quiet. I'm busy."

The chain and padlock clanked against the wrought-iron door pulls of the door to the forlorn building as Sabine jerked at the doors with no luck. She dug her fingers under the boards covering the glass and came away with a splinter. Cursing under her breath. She circled to the shutters that were nailed shut.

The peeling paint and splintered wood showed the rot of time. But when she tugged at them, they were strong as iron. Peeking through a crack, she could just make out the dusty interior. Motes floated in a sliver of sunlight that had seeped through the shutters. Broken glass lay across the floor. Most of the chairs were atop tables, but some had fallen haphazardly like passed out guests.

That woman had walked straight in. Maybe she was a ghoul? Sabine shook her head. No, she wasn't. Sabine would know a ghoul if she saw one. She was almost sure she would. Probably.

Letting out a fresh string of curses. Sabine hammered her fist against the shutter. For just a moment, the doors were flung open, neon danced inside, and the room was filled with jazz. Just as quickly, it was gone.

Sabine stepped back to get a clearer view. Everything looked just as destitute as it had when she first arrived. "How did that stretched out human get into an enchanted bar? I have more magic in my pinky toe than she has in her—"

An idea popped into her head. Digging through her satchel, she found the charm bracelet and slipped it around her wrist.

Nothing changed.

Sabine jangled it in front of the closed shutter.

Nothing.

"Stupid piece of trash." Although, it did sparkle nicely in the sun. "If a charmed bracelet didn't get her in, then how?" Stupid goblin giving away a charmless bracelet.

A harsh cackle came from the corner.

She spun around, looking for the infernal crow, the perfect target for her frustration. Instead, a grizzled man with spittle in his beard and uncombed hair let out another harsh caw of a laugh.

"You saw it, didn't you? I'll have to fix that, or Miss Zula de Bonaire will be coming after me. She don't like holes in her wards." The man stopped to pick a few crumbs from his mustache and deposited them in his mouth. He chewed on them thoughtfully as Sabine stood by, gaping.

"What do you know about this place?"

"I know I gotta fix that baby witch-shaped hole I left in the ward. That's what I know."

"I'm not a baby witch," Sabine muttered.

The grizzled man squinted and slowly walked toward her.

Sabine refused to move.

As he approached, the grooves in his face smoothed out. His crinkled eyes sparkled with youth. His whiskers shrank into a tidy hipster beard. His tangled hair darkened. He ran his fingers through it and it fell in dark waves around his cheeks.

"You're—" Sabine started.

"I know," he said, "rakishly handsome."

"What happened? What did you do?"

The proud, sharply dressed young man prowled past her. "Baby," he said, "witch."

"Well, you're a—"

The man just chuckled and walked on without a concern for what Sabine might think he was.

Craunk. The creeper crow settled on a door pull and set to picking at the worn wood. It cocked its head and gave her an I-told-you-so look with that beady little eye.

Sabine scowled, Thibodeaux style. "Where would he go next?"

Squawk.

"I'm not looking for the detective. I'm trying to help." Her voice sounded juvenile, even to her own ears.

Baby witches shouldn't play at grownup games, the crow squawked.

Sabine glared. "Baby witch might need a stuffed bird to play with."

Craaw, Craaw, Craaw!

Chapter 16

MEGAN

The door shut on her Buick, encapsulating Meg into the quiet interior. The sound of traffic, of the cars coming and going, of all the questions, they all receded. The officer who had escorted her to her car gave a curt nod and patted the roof twice, an indication that she was released.

Meg sat numb at the wheel. Where was she supposed to go? Carmichael had given her a list of inexpensive hotels in the surrounding area and left her with a warning not to leave the city. So, without a job, without a bunch of spare cash, Meg was supposed to rent a room to stay in while her paid for apartment sat empty.

Bullshit.

However, when she tried to picture going back to the cottage where she'd found her roommate, dead on the couch, Meg's muscles contracted involuntarily, and she gasped for air. Triggered by the sudden movement, a face appeared at her window. She jerked back with a yelp. The officer who'd escorted her to her car mouthed the words 'you okay?'

Meg nodded.

She was as okay as she could be for someone not allowed to leave this sinister city. As okay as she could be without her best friend to process the grief with. As okay as she could be with no memory of how it all happened.

With no job. No place to stay. And orders not to leave.

What more did they want from her?

They had all the answers Meg had to give. She'd recited everything that her memory supplied her. Everything from their decision to room together in New Orleans. To moving in a rental truck and a Buick. To going out to celebrate. The French Market. The walk to the bar. Then coming home and finding Valdi dead.

But when they questioned her in detail, Meg didn't have enough answers to fill in the gaps. Important ones.

Who had they seen at the market? Meg didn't know.

What had they bought at the market? Meg didn't know.

The name of the bar they went to afterward? Meg didn't know.

Nothing? Well, the name was something like 'night' or 'dark' and something about music. Yeah. The Midnight Jazz Club.

Where was it? *There*, she'd pointed at a paper tourist map.

On a laptop, they pulled up Google Map's street view. It was an abandoned building. Meg's ears buzzed. She couldn't get enough air.

"Could it be, like, one of those raves that opens and closes in one night in an abandoned building?" she asked, realizing how ridiculous she sounded, but she'd seen them on TV. She'd heard about them on the Internet. They must happen somewhere. If somewhere, why not New Orleans?

"You've been to these raves? You and Valdi?" No, Meg shook her head. She hadn't.

"And you know about them. How?" What was she supposed to say?

"TV. The Internet." Carmichael had nodded as she took notes. Meg was sure the officer scribbled *lies, lies, lies* on her pad.

"Who did you see in this bar that had a name like night and music?" Which is every bar in New Orleans, Meg thought.

"A cool man," she said it before thinking how useless the comment was.

Carmichael didn't seem disturbed. She just continued to prod. "Can you describe this cool man?"

Meg couldn't. She couldn't picture him. For a moment, she'd had an image of icy eyes, but when she tried to focus on them, the image slipped away. She thought he'd been sharp somehow. "His smile. He had a sharp smile."

Carmichael made more notes.

None of it made sense. Meg knew that. She knew Carmichael knew that. But there was no way Meg could think to repair the holes in her memory. Her breath caught.

Did That make her a suspect?

How could it not?

The sterile walls of the police office pushed in around her. She'd been offered a bitter cup of coffee, but the acid in her stomach was too strong to even consider more than a sip or two as she tried to ground herself in this horrific reality.

The officers questioning her had been polite and professional, but in between rounds of questioning, they darted furtive looks at one another. They didn't believe the story she told them. Which was fair enough. Meg didn't believe it either.

She'd studied the map. She'd put her finger on Café du Monde and slowly walked it down the streets until she reached the corner of Royal, where she was sure the bar must be. But they'd shown her no. No, it wasn't.

She'd walked the map up and down the street, hoping that on the next block, there it would be. But it wasn't.

Pulling out of the parking garage. Meg set the car's navigation to take her to one of the hotels. It told her to turn right.

Meg turned left. She cut down one street after another until she found herself back on Royal. She had to prove to herself what was going on.

What if Google Maps had an old image? Maybe it hadn't updated, and the building had reopened? Had the officers gone to check?

Driving down any street this close to the quarter was a pain under good circumstances. These were not good circumstances. Meg crept along with traffic. Her nerves vibrated just under her skin.

Almost there.

There.

It crouched. Sedate. Eyes shuttered.

Meg's joints grew numb. Her stomach soured. She'd hoped, without reason, that the police were wrong. That Google Maps was wrong. That her memory had just misplaced the bar by a block or two.

Her vision blurred so that she almost missed the stout woman laughing on the corner. Was that violet light glowing beneath her pale curls?

Meg slammed on the brakes.

A sedan rear-ended her.

The would-be Valdi was gone, replaced by a red fox dodging traffic.

The vocal car horn behind her told her exactly how big of an idiot she was.

Chapter 17

❖———————————————❖

SABINE

Assisting the tourists of New Orleans by sorting through their pockets, pouches, and purses was more of a chore and less of a game in the days that followed. Sabine passed a woman with delicate crepe skin emerging from an antique shop, a suppressed smile crinkling the corners of her eyes, her lips a tight. Before merging into the pedestrian traffic, she checked the contents of the stylishly plain brown gift bag she carried. As she did, her credit card slipped from her unclasped handbag, practically falling into Sabine's hand.

Without thinking it through, Sabine slipped the card back in and clasped the bag. When the woman turned in surprise, Sabine had already disappeared into the flow of people.

I don't fleece the innocent, Sabine rationalized, knowing nothing about the woman. Other than the delight on her face.

The following day, as the shops closed and the bar crowd emerged, a young man stumbled into her as he walked backwards, harassing a pair of women in full plumage. He spun and clung to Sabine to keep from falling. Her hand landed on the wallet halfway out of his back pocket. Instead of relieving him of it, she pushed it deeper in and shoved him off. He catcalled behind her as she continued on her way.

Not worth the effort, she reasoned, knowing her excuses grew more flimsy with each passing day.

Sabine's regular circuit past her aunt's house had changed without her permission. Instead of the familiar trek, she found herself passing the cottage where the stretched woman and her compact friend had lived. Neither returned home. One temporarily banished. The other dead.

The first night, once the police left, Sabine let herself back into the apartment to find what enchanted clues the sightless police had left. They had scoured the apartment for ordinary clues: bits and pieces of human residue, hairs and fibers, and fit bits. They took what they thought was relevant and left the rest for Sabine to rummage through for magical residue.

Nothing.

The second day, a cleaning crew in a white van marked BioClear arrived to remove any trace of the deceased from the attic apartment. Sabine watched from her perch in the oak. The couch and rag rug were declared a loss and hauled out for disposal. People in white coveralls and blue rubber gloves sanitized what was left.

The apartment remained dark and empty for another night.

The third day, lifeless.

Sabine allowed herself one pass by the detective's apartment to see why he was neglecting his duties. From the end of the block, she could see a light on. Sabine passed on the far side of the street. When she caught sight of a female silhouette behind the curtain, she continued to walk, scanning the trees and listening for an unsolicited crow's commentary on her actions.

None came, and she redirected to the second leg of her new circuit.

Where once Sabine had traversed the Greenwood Cemetery searching for signs of her late aunt lingering to offer support or guidance, now she traveled through St. Louis Cemetery, where she sought new residents, a compact shade studying her surroundings, perhaps. The shadows stretched long between concrete crypts. Clouds scudded across the waning moon. Shadows flickered uncertainly across the blank stone faces inhabiting the city of the dead.

Sabine was not afraid of the dead, but a traitorous part of her wished that infernal crow were around to keep an aerial view for her. She fell into fox form and loped through the gates that kept the wraiths contained.

The last leg of her circuit took her past the French market. It emptied itself of tourists and local vendors while Sabine sat on her fox's haunches and waited. No matter how hard she strained, she could not see the magical market opening.

Did it come every night? Was it just on the full moon? She barked in frustration.

Unfortunately, a fox's bark sounded eerily like a screaming woman and drew the attention of a janitor cleaning up. He froze, broom in hand, and listened. After a moment, he took a deep breath and made the sign of the cross before resuming his work.

Sabine passed behind a parked SUV as a fox and came out the other side as a young woman in an auburn jumper and matching slippers.

"What are you looking for, little witchling?" asked a large man. He could've been part bull if you squinted. Sabine narrowed her eyes to check. How had he snuck up on her?

"Arrived too late for shopping." Sabine shrugged and kept walking.

"Or a little too early. It opens again on the quarter moon."

"Thanks for the advice." Sabine wished she'd remained a fox.

The man eyed her warily.

She cut across the empty street. He followed.

She picked up her pace. The thud of heavy boots quickened.

She willed herself to remain calm. It didn't work.

She broke into a jog, and the thud of boots turned into the harsh clop of hooves. Darting a look over her shoulder, Sabine confirmed that it was the minotaur from the Faerie Market, and he was gaining on her.

Dropping into fox form, Sabine skittered underneath a dumpster and waited as the minotaur circled to the other side. Then she darted out, running at full speed. But he was ready. He overtook her and caught her rear leg and yanked hard.

Sabine yelped. Fire tore through her hip joint. The minotaur held her high, dangling over the asphalt, and glared into her eyes.

"You steal from the Faerie Market again, and I'll take it out of your hide."

Metal screeched as the minotaur forced the lid of the dumpster open. He tossed her, and Sabine sailed through the air. She hit the side and clawed at the metal sliding down, landing on the mound of garbage at the bottom. A swollen trash bag burst open beneath her, spilling day-old shrimp and grits, gravy and biscuits, jambalaya, all cooked into a noxious stew.

Sabine's ribs pumped like bellows as she tried to catch her breath. The minotaur's deep baritone laugh trailed off as he slammed the lid shut.

Sabine barked in anger and frustration. She jumped, hit the top, and was knocked back into the slime coating the bottom.

"Don't make me mess you up." The rumbling voice outside made several more varied threats before the clop of hooves receded.

Sabine paced over and across the mounds, searching for a way out before the trash trucks arrived in the early morning hours. Reluctantly, she shifted back into her human form and scraped shrimp tails and sausage bits from her hair. Standing on tiptoes, she could just reach the lid. She shoved. It swung open a couple of inches, then slammed back down. She shoved again. Again, it slammed shut. And again. Until she was breathless.

A rumble announced the arrival of a garbage truck. Its engine paused while hydraulic lifts whined, and metal screeched on metal. The dumpster thumped against the truck, emptying its load, and clanged against its concrete pad as it was set back down. Then the diesel engine revved, coming closer, one dumpster at a time.

At the far end of the container, a slice of light cut through the darkness. Sabine waded through knee-deep garbage to find a sliding door on the far end. She forced her fingers through the sliver of an opening and heaved. It screamed in protest and slid an inch before her feet slid from under her.

Sabine jumped back, faltered on her sore hip, righted herself, and heaved again. It slid several more inches. The metal vibrated under her hands and feet. She wedged herself through the opening and rolled out, falling into fox form on her way to the asphalt. She landed and scampered away as the dumpster rose over the bed of the garbage truck.

Running between the wheels as the truck rolled to a start, Sabine loped three blocks to plunge into the Jackson Square fountain to rid her fur of sour grits.

Chapter 18

THIBODEAUX

Sweat dripped down Jean-Luc's back and chest. The failing air conditioning sputtered in its death throes, unable to gasp out a cool breath of air. He soaked his undershirt in the sink, then wrung it out and washed the blood from his chin and neck. He rinsed the cloth until the water ran clear, then bathed his chest and back.

His suit coat hung on the back of the single ladder chair pulled up to the glass top dining table. His button-up shirt, part of his unofficial work wardrobe, was a loss, stiff with blood, too much to wash out. He wrung out his undershirt for the third time and draped it around the back of his neck.

He'd come in and out of consciousness over the past two days.

The first day after fully waking, he tried his phone, but its signal couldn't escape the dark fog swirling through the interior of the apartment. He nursed the battery, turning it off until shift change when the most officers were likely to be at the precinct to notice him missing and call. But no calls came.

On the second or third day, after he'd come to consciousness, the sun seeped through the black fog that lay across the room like a dense cloud of living shadows. A check of his phone had shown no missed calls or messages. So, he'd left it off to try again next shift change. His clothes had been plastered to him, still tacky with his own blood, a pool of sweat at his back. His tongue coated with a salty, metallic taste. His hair matted with it.

And that damn watch had lain beside him.

He'd put it back on the dresser where it had been when the police photographer documented the apartment. Jean-Luc didn't know if returning it had been the move of a professional or an accomplice. It had hummed beneath his fingers; the hands winding backwards at a frantic pace, as if it had been wound too tight, and the spring was in a hurry to release its tension. This was the least strange occurrence so far.

So he'd let the watch lie while he searched for a way out.

He'd tried nudging his way up to the spell on the door, only to be thrown back, knocking the breath out of him. Luckily, he didn't lose any more blood. He wasn't sure how much more he could lose. He already felt lightheaded.

Next was the window. He'd paced back and forth in front of it. The light leaking through gave no warmth, yet the apartment remained stubbornly stuffy from the day before. The heat was trapped by the black miasma that he walked through. Did it coat his lungs with pitch?

In an attempt to build up his courage, or talk himself out of it, Jean-Luc returned to the kitchen. The AC had given its last gasp, and the temperature in the apartment rose quickly. He guzzled two glasses of tap water, downed a protein bar, and reached for the last one before reconsidering. He'd better ration the scraps of edible food left. He woefully put it back in the otherwise empty box and turned back to his search for an escape.

Time to follow through with the plan to try opening the window. Or come up with a less dangerous alternative. He could lightly touch it, he reasoned, like a hot stove. If it threw him back . . . He looked around the apartment . . . He'd hit that chair or that table. He shoved both back before stalking up to the window, approaching it as if it were a water moccasin coiled and waiting for him.

One.

Two.

Three bracing breaths and he reached out with the tips of two fingers when a rattle came at the door to the corridor.

Jean-Luc jumped back as if he had been burned instead of merely startled.

The doorknob fidgeted, but didn't turn.

Was it Tyler Davis finally returning home?

The rattling stopped, and the door remained closed.

Jean-Luc caught himself on the back of a chair so his knees didn't hit the floor as the fresh adrenaline and the possibility of rescue drained away.

Then his ears perked to a new sound. The ticking of metal wire against metal tumblers. The scrape of a deadbolt sliding free. The clunk of the thumb lock turning in its cylinder.

The protector in him nearly yelled out for them to stop before they became trapped, too. But the survivalist in him crouched behind an armchair and waited as the door swung open to reveal a familiar face. The clever sneak thief.

Sabine.

A maelstrom of sensations flooded his already overly charged senses. First, before the flush of relief even, a sharp electric shock of terror stung his veins until she stepped through the doorway unharmed. Then came the cool release of tension. At last, someone to help.

"Sabine," he said with more emotion in his voice than was professional. "I can't believe I'm actually relieved to see you breaking into a crime scene."

She ignored him and surveyed the apartment coolly. Her eyes passed over him without stopping. He'd obviously hurt her feelings when he had her thrown out. Maybe he shouldn't have had her frisked.

But, damnit, she was a thief.

Not the time. He needed help to get out of there and keep her from being trapped, too. "Listen. Maybe I shouldn't have had Carmichael search you, but honestly, I thought you'd mind it less than if I did it."

The dark fog swirled around her as Sabine walked into the room, creating eddies behind her. Moving through the magic of the space—yes, he admitted it had to be some sort of magic—seemed natural to her.

Jean-Luc watched with a growing unease.

Had she done this? Was she that mad at him? She'd put the watch into his pocket.

His growing suspicion slipped when he noticed Sabine favoring her left leg. He almost asked what had happened when her brow creased, angry.

"I know you're pissed," he said. "I'm pissed, too, to be honest. You march onto a crime scene and start disturbing evidence—Look, I don't want to argue. I'm sorry for whatever offended you, but let me out of this now. I have a crime to solve."

Sabine limped across the room, disturbing only the odd mists, leaving everything else untouched. She didn't attempt to steal anything. She was just there to show her irritation. To show him she was in control.

"I know you're a thief. You know you're a thief. You can't blame me for doing my job. You can be pissed, but you don't keep my ass locked up in this apartment." Jean-Luc realized he'd made fists and relaxed his hands. He wasn't so much mad as he was . . . What? Betrayed.

"Magic is new to you, right? I get that. But this 'veil' of yours kicked my ass. I need stitches." He gestured to the blood seeping from the cut at his temple. She continued to ignore him.

"Sabine!" The throbbing pain and fear came out as a roar.

She seemed to answer him, but her words were muffled through the fog as she went into the bedroom, expecting him to follow. He did.

She talked some more. Again, her words were muffled.

He grabbed for her arm. She flinched. But when he closed his hand, it held only air. She stared straight into his eyes, squinting in concentration, then turned away. On her way out of the bedroom, she checked the chest of drawers.

Seeing what was on it, she smiled. Her mouth became soft and wistful. A surprising expression on that usually wry face of hers. She shifted her weight and winced, obviously hurt. His chest tightened.

"Sabine," he whispered.

She turned her head, frozen for a moment as if to catch the words. Then, the spell was broken, and she turned to leave.

Following close behind, he caught at her waist when she reached for the door. Even knowing the enchantment wouldn't harm her, still he feared for her. His arm passed through.

And she left.

Chapter 19

SABINE

A murder.

A missing person.

A surly Sabine who's not even thieving.

And still no sign of Detective Thibodeaux to take notice.

Having the flu and letting Carmichael check in on you is no reason to let all of New Orleans down. And by all of New Orleans, Sabine meant her.

He let her down.

Where was he when he should be there, scowling at her and demanding that she come up with an excuse he could accept to explain why her bloody fox prints were at the scene of a crime? To rail at her for dropping evidence into his pocket at another crime scene. And why was she searching for clues when she had no training?

Then begrudgingly asking for her help.

That was their compact.

He wasn't holding up his end.

By the fourth day after Thibodeaux's disappearance, Sabine found herself back at the first crime scene, picking the lock. She swung the door open and checked the frame for magic residue. As if she would even know what to look for. But she'd seen the veil across the door that day. She'd felt it. And warned Thibodeaux. After he threw her out.

It looked innocent enough in the daylight. So, she took a breath and stepped inside.

The door frame didn't nip at Sabine as she entered the apartment. She traced the edges for signs of the veil but found none. She gave the apartment a quick survey before entering further. She listened hard to the silence. Too quiet for an apartment. No AC blowing. No shuffling of feet from the apartment above. No sound of running water or warring neighbors.

Until . . .

Her ears tingled as if someone had blown into them. She twitched the feeling away.

"More ghosts?" she asked the empty room to fill the unnatural silence. She felt the tickle again, only lighter.

Perhaps it was remnants of the spell that'd been on the door before. She chose to ignore it and drifted lightly through the apartment like a wraith herself. Unsure of what she expected to find, nothing jumped out at her. Nothing that said the detective had lingered here.

Except . . .

In the bedroom, atop the chest of drawers, lay the pocket watch that she'd secreted into the detective's pocket.

Like a love note, said the crow. Only the feathered bag of bones wasn't there with her.

"No," she countered to the missing foul, "like a counter move in chess to say, 'Check.'"

Or 'I miss you.'

Sabine whirled in a circle on the toes of her slippers. No bird. Only the annoying memory of one. She'd been sure to shut the exterior door to keep it from following, yet it persisted in pecking at her thoughts.

To dislodge it, she worked through the meager clues she had. The detective had found the watch and, most likely, replaced it after the others had left. If he wanted it as evidence against Sabine, he would have taken it in with him. But Carmichael had said she hadn't seen him again that night. So, he must not have gone back to the office.

"He went home," she told herself. She resisted the urge to go back to his apartment that morning. It was too much like admitting she wanted to find him. Seeing a female's shadow in his window had filled Sabine's imagination with annoying images of Carmichael tending to an overly pleased detective. It was enough to twist her stomach, like sour milk in a latte.

But the missing man's apartment had been her last stop. With no sign of Thibodeaux, other than the replaced pocket watch, Sabine relocked the door and let herself succumb to the temptation to check Thibodeaux's apartment one more time, just to be sure he wasn't really down with the flu or with being shot or just being overly grumpy. She evaded the crow, not wanting to listen to its mutterings about her concern for the detective and his attention.

What she was really concerned about were the citizens of the Big Easy fending off crime on their own.

Except that wasn't true at all.

Sabine wasn't overly concerned about the stretched woman who'd obviously killed her compact roommate. Well, maybe she was. A little. She was just in a crabby mood. The detective's disappearance couldn't be the only reason. Could it?

"Enough," she told herself as she approached the building. Her hip still ached from her encounter with the minotaur, and she slowed her steps as she studied the apartment for signs of life. The detective's windows were dark. It might be empty, or Jean-Luc and Carmichael might be snuggled up in bed.

"I'll see who I see. And give him a piece of my mind while I'm there. And Carmichael, too, if she's around. They both owe me a thank you for all the leg work I've been doing."

Even if you've come up with zero new info?

"I discovered the wards on that building." Sabine climbed the stairs to Thibodeaux's apartment, her hip joint screaming.

You already knew that.

Sabine hesitated in front of Thibodeaux's door while she finished her argument with the imagined crow. Realizing she'd run out of responses, she knocked.

No answer.

"Should I knock again?" she asked the empty hallway.

Stop talking to yourself.

With a grunt of annoyance, she crouched and slipped two bent metal pins from her pocket. Within seconds, she was in the apartment. It smelled stale, as if no one had come or gone in several days. She tiptoed through the living area and peered around the open bedroom door. The bed was empty and crisply made.

Sabine limped silently into the bathroom before returning to check around the room. On the nightstand was a folded note. So, of course, she read it. The light coming through the window was enough to make out the words.

"Worried. Call when you get this."

"Why did ya feel the need to leave it by his bed?" Sabine asked the missing Carmichael, whom she was sure had left the note.

Unsurprisingly, the sour faced officer, who was not actually present, did not answer.

Coward.

Sabine would just have to take care of it all by herself. Nothing new about that.

"Worried. Call when you get this," she recited to herself. "You just call her while I get shit done."

Sabine knew where she needed to start.

Chapter 20

MEGAN

The coffee pod dribbled into the cup, and the toaster hummed as it toasted her frozen cinnamon swirl waffle. Otherwise, the apartment was silent. The owners downstairs were gone to work for the day. Meg had opened the windows to let in the morning birdsong, but even they had gone silent.

Her head rested against the upper cabinet as she breathed in the smell of coffee beans laced with French vanilla and the overly sweet scent of cinnamon and toasted bread. Her eyes closed, letting the sounds and smells fill her senses and flood out the intense emptiness of the apartment.

"They let you go back and live in a place after someone . . . Someone has been murdered there?" Meg had asked the officer who called to tell her the apartment had been released to be cleaned and re-inhabited.

"You don't have to go back if you have another place to stay. But, as previously requested, you are not to leave town until the investigation is complete."

"But I can go back? There?"

"Yes, we contacted your landlord earlier in the week to release them to hire a cleaning service. You're free to go home."

That is not home. Meg had ended the call and repacked the overnight bag, which she'd had to make last a week. Her motions were robotic as she tried to push the horrors of what waited her aside. The apartment had been cleaned. Her landlord had assured her when she called to confirm, thinking someone at some point would stop this madness.

Did everyone expect her to move back in and carry on with the life she had planned when that life had been severed in half?

Where else would she go? She still didn't have a job. Maybe she should have been looking for one instead of sitting in the hotel room ordering takeout with the blackout curtains closed. But she hadn't.

The vacuum created without Valdi in the apartment sucked at Meg's nerves, spreading them thin. She felt brittle enough that she might snap at the slightest touch.

The spring on the toaster released with a shot like gunfire. Meg jumped, banging her head on the cabinet. That's just what she needed right now, assault by a toaster. The coffee gurgled to a stop at the same time.

Taking her mug and the waffle, she headed to the bedroom, letting both singe her fingers.

The room still held two twin beds. Had they been meant for toddlers? Meg felt as lost as a five-year-old abandoned in the Big Easy without parental supervision. No one to tell her what to do next. Valdi had been the planner. Meg the dreamer.

Now, there was only the nightmare.

Warm air fluttered the curtains. They billowed like ghosts come to greet her. A face appeared behind them.

"Valdi?" Meg asked, afraid for they might answer.

"Nope. Afraid not." A petite woman with auburn hair perched in the open window. She bounded off the windowsill and crossed the room. Languid strides brought her right up to Meg until they stood almost toe-to-toe.

With this creature right under her nose, Meg was too scared to move lest the apparition notice her. Which was a bit ludicrous, because the apparition boldly stared up at her as confident as if she were a head taller instead of a half a head shorter.

Meg looked down without moving her head, fearing if she didn't to keep a watch on the woman she might shift into some sort of homicidal monster. As is, she didn't appear very threatening. Her eyes crinkled with intensity. And she seemed to hum with energy. Though her cunning smile did appear a bit wolfish.

How had she confused this tiny woman for Valdi? Her friend was rounded and calculating and dead. This woman was of the same height, but she was slight and intense and had a feral air about her, as if she might bite without provocation.

"You're not Valdi," Meg said like that might break the enchantment the tiny creature had over her.

"Nope, but I'm here to discuss her little adventure."

"She's dead. You call that an adventure?" Meg asked, emboldened by her rising anger. Nevertheless, she took a step back and held the coffee mug and rapidly cooling waffle as shields between her and the woman, just in case she might bite.

"You and I need to take a little tour," the petite woman announced as she stalked past Meg and headed toward the living room. The swish of her auburn ponytail nudged something in Meg's memory.

"Do I know you?"

"We met in the Faerie Market. I told your friend to walk away. It seems she didn't listen." The woman stirred through the knickknacks Meg and Valdi had placed on the entry table to make it look homey. "And I told her that goblin was dealing in mischief, not jewelry, yet you still walked away with this." She jingled a gold chain filled with charms on her wrist.

Meg bristled. "What makes you think I'm going anywhere with a thief who broke into my apartment?"

"Open window," the woman said in a sing-songy voice that irritated Meg, thankfully bringing down her fear and grounding her.

"Who are you? And why are you here?" Meg's shoulders tightened as her aggravation spiked.

The petite woman twirled on her slippers and faced Meg, which oddly set her on edge again, even though she was sure she could break the small woman in half if she needed to, unless she bit first. That sly smile crossed the woman's face again. "Oh, now you're curious about the company you keep. You sure weren't a week ago. Unless you're friendly with the Fae."

"Last week, I was a lot more stupid than I am this week. *This* week, I want to know who you are and why you're attempting to help." That's it. Hold the line. She can't order you around.

The woman threw her head back and groaned. "We're really going to do this?"

"Yes."

"I am Sabine," the woman snapped out. "Of the Domingue witches," she said with pride, as if Meg was supposed to know the name or believe her claims. This Sabine woman didn't seem to care. "I'm here because the police don't know what they're doing. Thibodeaux at least tried, bless his heart, but where is he?"

"Thibodeaux? I've heard that name. The cops were saying it. Is he some super sleuth or something?"

The tiny Sabine laughed. "Hardly. But he's a hell of a lot better than the rest. Have they done more than move the body and clean up?"

Involuntarily, Meg's eyes snapped to the empty spot where the couch used to sit. They roamed the floor where the rag-rug had soaked up most of the blood. Then to the slight stain, the cleaners couldn't quite remove from the hardwood floor. The overconfident Sabine walked with a slight limp, passing right over the stain on tiny feet as if she couldn't see it.

"Size five prints," Meg said to herself.

"What's that?" the woman snapped.

"You were here that night." Meg's face heated with fear, with confusion, with anger. "You killed her!"

"Wait. Wait." The little thief held up her hands, and miraculously, the charm bracelet had disappeared from her wrist. "I might have happened in after you went to sleep, but your friend was already a corpse by that point."

As her anger outpaced her fear, Meg began to feel her height advantage and paced across the room, ready to seize the woman by her throat.

Instead of showing fear, Sabine's smile grew wicked. Her eyes narrowed, and she stalked to the middle of the room to meet Meg in the spot where the couch once sat. Her expression was either a dangerous seduction, or the woman was considering pulling a switchblade on her.

Meg's breath caught. She knew that look. She'd seen it that night. At the bar. The inhuman movements. Images flashed in the air between them as the memories came in brief still pictures.

A cool face. Icy eyes. Hair of moonlight. A crescent moon dangling from a delicate ear. And teeth. Sharp teeth.

"You said fairies?" The question came out as a croak that burned Meg's throat.

"I said Fae." Sabine's eyes narrowed further, and a crease formed on her forehead.

"I think I met one."

"I bet you did."

There was that clever fox of a smile again.

Chapter 21

SABINE

Meg's lanky frame slumped towards Sabine as they stood in front of the abandoned building on Royal Street. Meg looked miserable to be there. The whole walk over, she'd mumbled that the cops assured her the club didn't exist, but her long strides meant she had some hope. Sabine quizzed her as she trotted to keep up.

Meg obediently picked through her tattered memories. "The police didn't believe any of it. *I* don't believe any of it." Meg had folded in on herself when they turned the corner and came within sight of the building.

Silly, sightless people. Only believe in what they see.

"I believe," Sabine said, with the assurance of one who believed in many things that she couldn't see. There were definitely too many that she couldn't.

"That just makes you as crazy as me," Meg muttered. With a defeatist sigh, she came to a stop.

Sabine left her and wove between the scarce early morning tourists. She stopped on the adjacent corner, sticking to the shadows beneath the awning in the hope that whatever inhabited the abandoned building wouldn't notice her approach. Out of the corner of her eye, she saw Meg come up behind her.

"Why do you need me? I can't see anything but a dump. I must have been too drunk and on the wrong street, but I can't find it anywhere."

Sabine squinted at the building, attempting to force a vision of what lay beneath. "I need you for this," she said, dipping her hand into her leather satchel and drawing out the charm bracelet. "Put it on."

"I'd rather not." Meg had gotten more irritable, having the specter of her dead friend back in the apartment.

"It won't work for me. I tried it," Sabine admitted begrudgingly.

This caught the woman's attention. She cocked her head, gave the building a wary glance, then slipped the bracelet over her hand. "It didn't have charms when he gave it to me. I don't know where they came from or why he wanted me to have it so bad."

"He's a goblin. My momma said they have their own wants and wishes, and a witch is hard pressed to guess what they are."

"What?"

"Forget it. What do you see?"

"Nothing," Meg said without looking up. "Do you really believe that stuff about witches and goblins?"

"I know about witches. And I'm assuming my momma didn't lie to me about goblins."

"Maybe we should get your mother to help."

"She's dead."

"I'm sorr—"

"Just jingle it at the building or something."

"Why?" Meg studied the crescent moon charm intently as if it held some answer.

"Well, I know your friend saw her way in because I gifted her those faelight earrings. I'd hoped she see sense and stay away from the market and places like this. But apparently, your friend was a fool."

"She was no fool. She was brilliant and practical. Maybe a little obsessive about dissecting new things. You don't know anything about her or me or police work. You think you're a witch, for God's sake." Meg straightened, and Sabine could sense she was about to turn and leave, but something caught her eye, and she stood gaping instead.

Sabine turned and stared. Her eyes burned from the effort, but she couldn't see anything different. "What're you seeing? Tell me."

"It's full on night," she said, then looked around at the rest of the street, "but it's not."

"Yep, that's the In Between. I knew it. Here," Sabine grabbed Meg's hand and laced their fingers together.

"What are you doing?"

"Experimenting."

"You don't really know much about this magic stuff, do you?" Meg asked, but her eyes were wide and focused on the neon sign over the door.

"Midnight Jazz Club," Sabine read. The sky over the club was blue-black and studded with stars, more than could be normally seen from inside the city at night, or during the day, for that matter. The upper floor of the building was dark, but not dilapidated. Moonflowers twined in and around the balustrade. The first floor was ablaze.

Jazz poured out French doors thrown open to the sidewalk. Fantastic and fearsome creatures danced and mingled within the walls, ignoring the street on the outside. Sabine thought the woman behind the bar looked like the same one who'd slipped through the wards the day after the murder.

"I knew it!" Meg squeezed her hand until it hurt.

"Didn't sound like it," Sabine muttered and pulled her hand back, but the image flickered out. She took Meg's hand again while the woman gaped at the Fae nightclub. This was going to be awkward.

"The moon charm. The crescent. It looks kind of like the one a man wore here. The one who asked me to dance. The tall one with the light hair and cold eyes."

Sabine cut her gaze from the Fae to Meg. She'd just described at least a fifth of the club. "Does the charm look like the one he wore, or *is it* the one he wore?"

Meg examined it again. "Why would I have his earring?"

Sabine flipped her hand back and forth, trying to conjure up an easily understandable answer. "Fae like to acquire and distribute trinkets like, sort of, tokens, souvenirs, or kind of trophies."

"Like serial killers keep?"

"No. Well. Not . . . Yeah, maybe. And you should never accept one unless you're pretty sure they'll kill you or eat you if you don't."

"*Or* eat you?"

"Yeah, sometimes it's both/and, sometimes it's either/or." Sabine could feel they were getting too deep into minutia that she wasn't willing or able to answer. "Doesn't matter. You've got it now. Let's go in and see if we can find this moon man."

Meg looked skeptically at the building. "I don't think that's a safe plan."

"Oh. It's definitely not," Sabine said, clenching their linked hands and dragging the stretched woman into the Midnight Jazz Club.

Chapter 22

━━◆━━

CARMICHAEL

At least one officer had been on watch for Ms. Megan Armand since she left the precinct. It hadn't been much of a chore while the woman stayed holed up at the hotel Carmichael had suggested. She kept her curtains drawn, and no one came or left for a week other than food delivery. Once, she'd left the room to request toothpaste at the front desk, but otherwise, she sat tight.

Carmichael couldn't make out what the woman's game was. Why kill her roommate? Why make up such a half-ass story? The crime had obviously been impulsive. No planning, then a hysterical call to the police. It should make it all easier to work out, but Carmichael couldn't help feeling like she was missing the big picture.

She knew was her dependency on Detective Thibodeaux. He'd had a good instinct for this sort of odd crime. He'd see just beyond what the simple evidence showed.

Then there was that little snarky woman that he let trail around after him. Thibodeaux knew she was a criminal. Small time, sure, but still a criminal. A niggling voice in the back of her head asked Carmichael if Thibodeaux and the woman were in league somehow, and that's how he solved unsolvable crimes. Carmichael felt disloyal for even thinking it. She wrote the suspicion off, blaming her police training to ask questions and suspect everyone.

The detective was a good man. A better person than she, Carmichael thought. That tiny red-head was trouble, but it was petty street crime. What Carmichael had done . . . It didn't violate any crime on the books, but that didn't make it right, and she knew it.

Shaking off her latent guilt, she followed Megan down the sidewalk as she returned to the scene of the crime, as they say. The building where she'd said they met the strange man. The tall woman was easy to follow, particularly in the early morning when the tourist traffic was at its thinnest. Even in a crowd, Megan stood several inches above most of the others.

Carmichael did have a hard time tracking Megan's new companion, perhaps her accomplice, a slight woman whose hair shone like copper when the sun hit it. She came and went with the shadows in an unnatural way. Carmichael told herself it couldn't be that petty thief, but who else moved like that?

Carmichael knew that she held a grudge against the slippery thief for following her into the missing Tyler Davis's apartment unnoticed. She'd caught a glimpse of a large cat on the stairs, but had been sure there was no person other than her. She was good at her job, and she knew it. She didn't need Thibodeaux for this.

The suspect literally had blood on her hands when they arrived at the scene. Sure, she'd been distraught, but you could care about somebody and still kill them. Carmichael knew this for a fact. Why the chief didn't think they should lock up this Megan character, Carmichael didn't know. Maybe he didn't trust Carmichael's opinion like Thibodeaux did.

Or like he pretended to.

No, he *did*, she assured herself. Now, focus.

The little thief took the tall woman's hand and dragged her across the street. They seemed to disappear into the corner entrance of the abandoned building, although the doors were chained shut. They must've turned down the side street.

Carmichael radioed Officer Johnson, who was assisting her that afternoon. He followed one block north in case the suspects pulled some shit like this. The walkie-talkie rasped to life, and the accompanying officer replied.

"They didn't turn this way, sir." Johnson often slipped and addressed Carmichael with a "sir." She never corrected him. They weren't on a battleship, but Carmichael felt it established her authority over him, even if by accident.

"Keep a watch. They must've seen one of us." If they'd seen either of the officers, it would have been Carmichael. Johnson had a full block between him and them. But she couldn't bring herself to claim responsibility for letting herself be spotted and losing line of sight. "They'll surface from one of these buildings. Hold tight."

"On it, sir. Uhm, ma'am." Johnson fumbled the last. Maybe he was catching on. Too bad.

"Diane, head this way. Across from the designated building." Carmichael said to the officer who had followed on the block just south. She reflexively referred to her female cohort by her first name, while she referred to Johnson by his last. She knew what she was doing. She could stop it. But she didn't.

The officer joined her, jogging around the corner. So eager to comply. Carmichael wondered if she came across that desperate to Thibodeaux. She signaled for Diane to slow down before she was noticed. Diane's face flushed, either from running in the heat or being called out for running in the heat. Didn't matter. Carmichael gave her a Thibodeaux grade scowl, or attempted to. The other woman shifted on her feet.

"You'll learn," Carmichael told her, throwing her a bone while also making sure she understood that Carmichael was her superior. "What did you hear this morning?"

Diane straightened her shoulders, ready to report. Such a junior move. Carmichael had ordered Diane into the office to get the latest reports back from the lab while Carmichael check back at Thibodeaux's apartment. Her note had lain right where she'd left it. The apartment looked unchanged.

Where was he? And was he coming back?

"The lab reported official cause of death was exsanguination." Carmichael must have looked confused, because Diane quickly filled in the blanks. "Death by blood loss."

"Of course," Carmichael snapped. "We saw that. Blood all over the place."

"Except there were no visible wounds, and she didn't appear to have bled from any orifice. No needle marks were found."

"Was the blood on the floor hers?"

"Yes."

Carmichael would have appreciated a 'yes, ma'am', but the officer's discomfort would have to do. "Then how did the blood get from *inside* the body to *outside* the body?"

"The medical examiner says he has no idea."

"What am I supposed to do with that?" A growl rose in Carmichael's throat. How did everything magically fall into place for the detective, but the moment he goes missing, nothing makes sense anymore? "Anything *useful* from the lab?"

"Yes." Diane brightened like a kid with a good grade on their rudimentary spelling test. "First, the prints outside the apartment were definitely made by a fox, not a dog. The blood was a match with the victim. And some info on that guy Detective Thibodeaux was looking into before he," she hesitated before saying 'he went missing,' and continued with. "Well, the one whose disappearance he was investigating a week ago."

"Let's hear it. I need something." Carmichael said, but she was barely listening. Something shimmered at the corner of the building, like metal oil canning in the meager light under the awning, except the doors were covered in plywood.

"We have pictures of Tyler Davis leaving town in a vehicle reported stolen. Caught on a traffic cam on the Lake Pontchartrain bridge, the day before he was reported missing. I left the folder on your desk."

"Good. Good." Carmichael said absentmindedly.

"Ma'am, have you heard anything from Thibodeaux?"

"No," Carmichael said. And she wondered if she ever would.

Chapter 23

MEGAN

An older Creole man served glasses of deep violet and pale periwinkle from taps behind the copper bar. Elegant creatures accepted the tall glasses with languid, dismissive motions before flowing back into the crowd on the dance floor. Melancholy music wailed from a single sax on a platform in one corner while the patrons swayed like seaweed in a current.

Curious and ominous gazes scanned Meg and the sly little Sabine just in front of her. Meg's shoulders rolled in as if she could make herself smaller, and she scooted further behind the thief.

"Don't let them sense your fear," Sabine said.

"They can feel it?" That didn't help Meg's nerves at all. "How? Like a snake sniffing the air with its tongue."

Sabine's attention snapped back to her. The petite woman's mouth worked as if she were sampling the taste of the words before spitting them out. "Yeah, that's an amazingly astute description. Keep that serpent image in mind, and maybe you won't get bitten."

A memory struck of a razor sharp pain lancing her ear, and Meg said, "I think it might be too late for that."

The sly woman's eyes roved over Meg as if looking for obvious wounds. Finding none, she asked, "Does anyone here look familiar?"

The crowd no longer watched them, yet the hairs on Meg's arms bristled as if she were being sized up for a meal. The creatures looked nearly human, but not quite human enough to be right. What did they call that? "The uncanny divide?"

"The uncanny valley," Sabine responded, obviously reading the room the same way Meg did.

Skin tones ranged from pale to dark, but not in a normal array of hues. The woman with milky pale skin actually looked as if her skin were liquid cream and not flesh. The young man with a dark brown complexion had a rough texture, as if it would feel like bark to the touch. The bass player's skin was like an oil slick, reflecting a rainbow sheen where the light struck it.

Hairstyles ranged from bald to floor-length braids, which was not all together strange for New Orleans. But the dancer with fins on either side of their head like a crown—now that was disturbing. And those with swept back hair all had oddly pointed ears. Pointed like a canine. Pointed like a bat. Or pointed and tufted like a feline.

"Nothing here looks familiar at all. Is this some sort of fetish bar?" Meg asked, hoping it was.

Sabine hesitated before shrugging. "You could say that. Just not too loud. Or they might take it as an invitation."

Her every word served to unnerve Meg even more. "Maybe we should go get the cops."

"Did they believe you when you told them this was a bar?"

"No," Meg said sullenly.

"Who believed you?"

"You did."

"Exactly. So, we're doing this together," Sabine said.

"You never told me why you're helping."

"Because I—" The clever woman fumbled over her words. "It doesn't matter. I'm here. I'm helping. Now, please tell me if you recognize anyone at all."

Meg tried to survey the crowd without lifting her chin from her chest. Luckily, she was tall enough that this worked surprisingly well.

"Him. The older man behind the bar."

"Come on, then." Sabine dragged her through the crowd.

No one seemed to notice the tiny woman pushing them aside, just Meg begging forgiveness while hurtling along behind her. Both growls and purrs followed in their wake. As they reached an opening at the bar, the saxophone ended on a wistful note that lasted long after the musician had lowered his instrument.

"Sounds more bluesy than jazz, don't you think?" the sly Sabine asked the man behind the bar.

"Give it a minute," he said.

This Creole man with laugh lines at the corners of his warm eyes looked fully human. Thank God. He lifted his gaze from the glass he'd been drying, and a green fire flashed from deep within his pupils.

Okay. Almost fully human.

Sabine took in a breath to speak, but a trumpet blared, launching an urgent syncopated song. The room broke loose. Dancers moved like trees tossed about by a storm. The sound drowned out Sabine's words, but the bartender nodded. He yelled over his shoulder, loud enough to be heard over the music.

"Boss Lady, someone's here for you."

At the far end of the bar, a young woman with a curly fro and warm skin flipped her wrist, a gesture to let him know she'd heard. After topping off two glasses, one with an amber liquid, the other with a rose-colored concoction, she headed their way.

"So, you're the boss lady?" Sabine asked. The woman shot a withering look at the Creole man, who grinned and went to take over her customers at the far end.

The barkeep shook her head and snorted. "Sure. What is it you need?"

Her gaze skimmed over Sabine's head to Meg, and Sabine pulled her forward. She loomed over the barkeep. The top of the barkeep's fro was at Meg's eye level, even as Meg slouched out of habit. Meg felt like she might recognize this woman, too. She looked mostly human. A spectacular one, but a relatively normal spectacular as compared to her clientele.

"I, uhm, think I've been here before. Not that you would remember me. I just—"

"I remember," the woman said.

"Okay, yeah, but I don't, really. I sort of remember coming in with my friend, then, well, not much after that."

The barkeep put a glass of a daffodil yellow liquid in front of Sabine without looking at her. Sabine took a sip, and her eyebrows shot up in appreciation.

"That'll be ten dollars. Human dollars, no enchanted paper. Thank you."

Storm clouds started brewing in Sabine's expression, so Meg yanked out her wallet and gave the woman a twenty. Not that she had cash to spare, but she needed them to stay on topic.

"Can you tell me what you remember? Like who my friend and I might have talked to?" Meg asked.

She snorted in reply. "Talked to? The Fae do love their mysteries." The barkeep swiped the money off the counter and replaced it with a ten. "You're lucky. They liked you. Check your charms. Chances are they left the memories there. Otherwise, they're gone, and I can't fill them in for you."

"Can't or won't?" Sabine asked, keeping a tight grip on Meg so that she couldn't lift her arm to check the bracelet.

"All the same here," the woman answered as Meg tugged to release Sabine's locked arm. How was such a tiny beast so strong?

"Could I take a look?" Meg asked, nodding to her wrist.

Sabine glared at her as if she'd asked to politely rip her arm off. After looking down to see what Meg was going on about, Sabine relented and brought their joined hands up to eye level, Sabine's eye level.

"You're saying all her memories are stored in these?" Sabine sounded skeptical.

"I said they might be," the barkeep corrected her. "They might also contain an enchantment that will cause her to seek the giver mindlessly without stopping for food or sleep until she perishes, or cause her to speak in tongues forevermore, or a wicked binding spell so that she can never release her grip."

Upon hearing this last one, Sabine snatched her hand back from Meg and looked at her accusingly as if she'd been trying to entrap her. She flexed her fingers. "Well, go ahead, check that moon one you were going on about."

"What if it makes me howl at the moon or turn into a werewolf or both?" Meg held her wrist out in front of her, suddenly frightened of the gifted bracelet.

"You said the guy who gave it to you was cool and pale. That doesn't sound like a warm-blooded werewolf."

"I also said he had sharp teeth. Lots of them."

"True. But I'm partial to canines." Sabine clasped the dangling moon against Meg's wrist and held it firm under her thumb. "Remember anything now?"

Meg shook her head as a cool hand snaked around her waist. Icy fingers brushed the skin between her shirt and the waistband of her jeans. She shrieked.

A pale man, several inches taller than her, with hair like moonlight, and skin so pale it appeared almost blue, hugged her to his side and gave her a sharp smile in greeting. "It's been several human days, has it not? I assumed a lesser Fae held your attention. Yet here you are."

Bringing her hand to his cool lips, he brushed a kiss across her knuckles. It burned like the first singe of frostbite. He tilted his head and whispered into her ear. "The first charm is always the best, don't you think?"

Sabine stood with hands on her hips, and eyes narrowed. "I can still see you. How come I can still see you?"

"Witches have a way of worming their way in where they aren't wanted." The man turned to Meg, dismissing her companion.

"I couldn't see any of you before. Not unless I had contact with Meg, and she wore the bracelet." Sabine's words were barely audible over the music.

As Meg considered how to extract herself from this man's grip and whether that was actually what she wanted to do, the barkeep turned her full attention to Sabine.

"Once the Midnight Jazz Club lets you in, you can stay until it expels you. Those two will be at it for a while, if the other night was any indication. Do you want another drink?"

"What happened the other night?" Meg asked the cool man with the sharp smile. He'd dipped his face in so close that her lips brushed against his as she spoke.

"You were a very busy girl." His teeth grazed her lips. Meg tasted the tang of blood. "A very busy, very naughty girl."

His pupils grew wide and deep and dark. Meg felt herself tip forward, losing herself inside them.

Chapter 24

SABINE

That damned blue Fae nearly swallowed poor, naïve Meg whole. The two were in full make out mode in front of the bar while jazz wailed over the dance floor. The Fae lining up to be served appeared oblivious, or unconcerned, about their cohort nearly swallowing a female whole. The barkeep ignored the incident and continued serving drinks.

"Back off, Papa Smurf." Sabine punched the Fae in the shoulder to no effect. She circled around and tore Meg free of his grip. "Snap out of it."

Meg grabbed the bar for support, breathless, face flushed, while Sabine glared at the male, daring him to come at Meg again. He gave her a lazy smile full of sharp teeth, but kept his distance. So, Sabine turned her ire on the woman behind the bar.

"You weren't planning on stepping in to stop him?"

"It's not my place to intervene with consenting adults." The barkeep said while filling glasses and collecting money, with no concern for her clientele consuming mortals.

"She was *not* consenting. He had her under some sort of thrall." The male chuckled at Sabine's accusation. "Tell them, Meg."

Instead of backing her up, the strangely tall woman had the nerve to blush and duck her chin.

"Really?" Sabine asked, disgusted. Meg tipped her head in the universal acknowledgment of 'Yeah, I was into it.' "Dead roommate. Remember? Blood everywhere. Concentrate."

At least Meg had the decency to look ashamed. "It's hard to focus here."

"Maybe you ladies should leave. This is no place for mortals," the barkeep said before moving to the far end to help.

Sabine ignored the warning. She was no mortal. Well, she actually *was* mortal. Her mother and aunt had died so, technically, she could die, but so could immortals. And she was a witch, albeit one with little knowledge of the whole witching thing. But still. She was offended to be grouped with Meg.

"So, these little charms, you just touch one to activate it, and boom, Papa Smurf here?" Sabine asked. The pale Fae's eyes narrowed, hard and sharp as ice cycles. "Were you with Meg all night the night you met? Did you pass her around to your Fae friends? Did you see the other human? Who was she with? Who did she leave with? Did she leave with you?"

"Sabine!" Meg stopped her.

Was Sabine the only one who wanted to take care of business?

"What?" she asked. "He looks pretty shady to me."

Meg's cheeks flushed. "I remember that night. Or parts of it."

"You just suddenly remembered. Just like that." Sounds suspicious to me. Sabine thought, but didn't say. Although she felt sure, her tone conveyed it just fine.

"The kiss, it must've broken the memory loose."

"I'll bet it did." Sabine wondered if maybe Meg and this blue man had leagued up to kill her roommate. Probably not. Meg seemed despondent. Not guilty, despondent, more like my friend is dead and I have to pay all the rent myself, despondent. Mr. Freeze, on the other hand, he was definitely coldhearted enough to pull it off.

Meg cut her eyes to Mr. Freeze, then at her feet. "Valdi took off through the crowd while we danced."

"Did you see her again before leaving?"

"I can't quite remember that part."

"Were you with this guy all night?"

"I, uh, yeah. Him and another guy."

"Another guy?" Sabine asked, incredulous. Not that she didn't know about these things, but Meg did not seem the type to explore multiple partners at once. "What were you up to with these two guys?"

Meg turned beet-red, which was odd for a woman shaped like a stalk of celery. "I'd rather not say."

"Well, you're going to have to tell the police something."

"Am I?"

"Excuse me?"

"Think about it. You're the one that reminded me the police didn't believe the bar existed. And it was you who pointed out that you couldn't get in without me and the bracelet. If I go to them with this story of two Fae and me doing—" She choked on the last bit. "Trust me. They'd only be more suspicious."

"The police already know you're keeping things from them," Sabine said, but knew it was true. There was only one officer who would listen. He wouldn't believe it, not really, but he'd listen and might be able to dig some relevant information from Meg's Fae affair to find the murderer. But he was still missing in action.

Meg folded in on herself again. Mr. Freeze ran a hand down her arm and leaned in to whisper in her ear. She looked hopeful, then back to despair when he melted into the crowd after giving Sabine a sharp look.

"What was that for?" Sabine called after his retreating form, but he'd already blended in with the mass of bodies moving on the dance floor. "Creepy bastards come and go right under everyone's noses and think they can get away with anything."

"Because they usually do?" said the barkeep. "Zula, Zula de Bonaire, I own the bar. And it's time the two of you headed out before anyone gets in trouble. I can't run a bar and babysit humans at the same time."

"Babysit? I don't need babysitting," Sabine said as the barkeep headed off again to tend to a line of patrons. She looked around to take her irritation out of the only other human in the bar, but Meg was already halfway to the door.

"How did two humans get jewelry that let them into the In Between, anyway?" Sabine muttered to herself. Other than the earrings which Sabine had given the dead woman. Purely for defensive purposes, not to take herself into enemy territory.

"Ask the goblin who gave her the bracelet," a warm breeze spoke directly into her ear.

Sabine spun around, expecting to find Mr. Freeze. No one was there, but the Creole bartender smiled at her from behind the bar. Sabine darted a glance to the retreating Meg, then leaned over the bar and asked. "So, this Boss Lady of yours, Zula, she seems human. Could she possibly be, you know, a witch?"

His eyes crinkled, emphasizing the laugh lines. "Miss Zula is one of a kind. But she's close with the Bayou Hag. You need to talk to someone about your little magic problem, chérie, you come back here sometime. I'll put in a good word for you."

"I don't need to talk to anybody. And I don't have a problem, magic or otherwise."

Sabine could've sworn she heard that damned crow cackling at her.

Outside, she found Meg gulping down mouths full of stardust coated air. The neon Midnight Jazz Club splashed watercolor light over the street, painting it like an oil slick.

Meg frantically searched left and right, forward and back.

"Meg." Sabine tripped to a stop so that she didn't run into her. "We have to go back to the Faerie Market and talk to the goblin who gave you that bracelet."

"You go where you want," Meg said, still trying to catch her breath and orient herself. "I'm going back to the apartment. I'm going to convince the owners to break the lease. And then I'm getting out of this city."

"You can't."

"I can, and I am."

Sabine couldn't go back there alone. She started ticking off reasons on her fingers, feeling a bit desperate. "First, the police didn't say you could leave, did they? Second, it's night. You're not talking to anyone in the middle of the night except the goblin."

"What do you mean, night?" Instead of searching the streets, Meg began searching the skies. The one directly over the Midnight Jazz Club was star-studded, just as it had been when they went in. The sky beyond was not the cool blue of a coastal morning. Instead, it bled from the inky black of midnight to the blue-black of twilight.

"It was morning when we went in," she said to Sabine accusingly, as if she'd caused this anomaly.

"They said the bar was in the In Between. Places like that don't work the same. We can't even be sure it's the same day."

"It's the same day, just not the same time," a deep baritone spoke from behind Sabine.

She yelped like a startled canine.

They both turned to find a tall man with startling green eyes. He was even taller than the cool man. Meg craned her neck to look up at him. He was very nearly human, but too handsome to be true.

His rugged face warmed into a comforting smile. "Zula sent me out to see that the two of you weren't bothered on your way out of the In Between."

"Well, we're out now. Or nearly so. So, no help needed," Sabine informed him.

The man's lips curled into a wry smile. "I'm sure you don't, small one. But allow me to walk you home to assuage my conscience."

Sabine jumped in before Meg could answer. "Your conscience is no concern of ours. Right, Meg?"

The handsome, fiery green eyes focused on Meg, inquiringly.

Meg shook her head at the man and Sabine both, and darted out of the pool of light cast by the sign and into the shadowed street.

"See what you've done?" Sabine barked at the man. She caught up to Meg and had to lengthen her stride to keep pace.

"The market. There has to be a reason you were given that bracelet," Sabine tried to convince her.

Meg stopped and bent over to put herself eye-to-eye with Sabine.

"Go away."

At that moment, a woman across the street caught her attention.

"What?" Meg asked.

"The police. Go home. I'll get them off our tail. Go."

She had the nerve to command Meg.

"I am. And you better not show back up."

Sabine didn't have time to stay and argue if she was going to draw attention away from the distraught woman. She took off in the opposite direction from Meg's apartment, sprinting. A glance back told her it worked. The officers were following.

Chapter 25

THIBODEAUX

The black mists drifted across the window as the sky sank into a bruised silence. From his position on the floor, Jean-Luc watched night overtake day once again. He sat in the bedroom of the missing Tyler Davis's apartment with his back to the abandoned chest of drawers. His legs stretched out in front of him. His boots discarded.

After Sabine's departure, the fourth day of entrapment, as far as he could tell, Jean-Luc gave up his frantic attempts to escape and took a shower. With no AC, showers were his only means of cooling off. It would take him another two days to get all the blood from under his fingernails.

By the fifth day, he gave up trying to call out and left his phone off. The carefully rationed saltines, stale chips, and frosted strawberry pop tarts were gone. He'd subsisted on water from the sink. And took brief naps on the couch between failed attempts to find new means of escape.

By the sixth day, he'd given in to fatigue and remained unconscious for most of the day.

The seventh had passed with him on the floor, holding the cursed watch as it ticked down the minutes backwards. The hands seemed to slow down as he watched, but it could just be his vision going out of focus. He could feel his heartbeat sync with the ticking.

At first, he'd resisted. But how does one control the beat of their heart?

In the end, Jean-Luc relaxed into it. Letting the timepiece count down his minutes until both it and his heart came to a halt. He closed his fingers over the glass face so he didn't have to see his life bleed away and studied the mists instead.

They seemed to slow as well.

His focus adjusted from the fog to the darkening sky, then back again, then drifted out of focus. As the hum of the watch numbed his palm, he focused once again on the Fog.

Then, the Sky.

Then Nothing.

The Fog.

The Sky.

Nothing.

Until there was no fog to focus on.

Jean-Luc slowly leveraged himself out of the slump he'd fallen into.

Was he delirious?

Leaning forward, he tried to catch the last tendrils of mist, like wisps of a tattered spider web, dissolving. He could no longer feel the ticking of the pocket watch. He braced himself and slowly unclenched his fist.

The hands on the watch face moved so slowly that he had to stare, unblinking, to be sure they moved at all. His eyes watered, and the minute hand climbed from nine to ten. He blinked them clear, and the sluggish hand crept past ten to eleven. After a hesitation, it ticked another second down. Jean-Luc held his breath through the next three.

The watch stopped one second from midnight.

His muscles ached, and his heart seized.

His breath solidified in his chest, too thick to flow.

His vision blackened at the edges.

It was lonely here at the end of time.

*

The hand snapped to midnight.

*

Everything broke loose.

Jean-Luc's heart raced as if trying to catch up to where it had left off. Air rushed from his lungs in a roar. He sprang to his feet and had to grab for the dresser as his knees threatened to buckle. Catching his balance, Jean-Luc practiced taking air in and letting it out.

"Slow. Take it slow," he cautioned himself, lest he move too quickly, and the watch restarted, and the mists returned.

Padding on bare feet, he found his boots by the bathtub along with his undershirt. He pulled it over his head, the neck catching at the stubble on his chin. Next, he located his socks in the living room with his suit coat. He slipped them on, then his boots, all without daring to sit. With frequent checks on the window for the mist's return, he strapped on his Glock 23 and tugged his coat over weakened arms.

Jean-Luc stretched his neck. Loosened his shoulders. Took a deep breath, and approached the door like a street brawler. If it attacked him this time, he'd likely die. But he had to try.

His fingers stroked the doorknob without recourse. He gripped the dented brass knob in a hard fist and turned. The tumblers released, and the door swung open.

Jean-Luc choked on a breath as it burst from his chest.

"Get it together," he told himself before stumbling through. In the corridor, he bent, hands on knees, dripping sweat. He was out.

Taking a deep breath, he looked back to his prison cell.

"What the hell!"

The apartment was ransacked.

Nothing like the apartment that he'd inspected with Carmichael and the lab techs. The oppressive fog had cleared, but the furniture was thrown against the walls, leaving a bare spot on the floor. Where no evidence could be found before, now the boards were coated with a rusty spray of dried blood. It trailed across the overturned coffee table and painted the white-washed wall with a gruesome portrait of a violent attack.

"One thing at a time," he said, his voice hoarse as he shut the door and headed home.

Chapter 26

MEGAN

Luckily, Sabine hadn't shown up at her apartment after the last trip to that mad bar full of creepy curiosities. Thank God. She didn't know if the police caught the thief. And if they had, what would they charge her on, breaking into what appeared to be an abandoned building?

They had nothing on Sabine.

Unlike Meg, who called the police, hands sticky with blood.

Meg spent the night after her second trip to the Midnight Jazz Club, sitting on her bed in the dark, staring at the window to be sure Sabine wasn't coming. While fiddling with the chain around her wrist, she relived the experience. Unlike the night with Valdi, Meg could remember every detail.

As Meg passed through the swarm of otherworldly creatures, flashes of memory had barraged her. The cool man's gaze from across the room left trails of icy fingerprints down her torso. A man with sharp ears tipped with tufts brought the sensation of warm, wet kisses up the side of her neck. A group, in a tight knot around a table next to the French doors thrown open to the night, watched her escape. Their gaze made her knees wobble. Her hands felt hot and tingly.

Without being able to grasp any of the particulars, Meg was overwhelmed with impressions when a shadow sailed across the window, startling her back to the dark bedroom at the top of the cottage. She tensed, waiting for a fox to appear. It didn't. Only the lonely cry of a crow searching for its companion.

Her fingers absently brushed a charm, and a mournful howl sounded outside, as if it were right under her window. She quickly let go and held her arm out, charms dangling away from her skin. The howling stopped.

She snatched the bracelet off, threw it onto the vanity, pulled the covers over her head, and didn't sleep a wink the rest of the night.

The next morning, she called the couple who owned the house. After wrestling with them for an unproductive two hours, Meg gave up on breaking the lease and leaving town. She did dedicate several hours that night considering how to get herself evicted. But the next morning, she went on a job hunt, then returned home with a rug from a thrift shop to cover the remnants of the bloodstain.

The second night, she braved another attempt at delving into her memories before bed. Meg turned the lights off first, hoping no one would realize she was home. She pinched the chain of the charm bracelet between her thumb and pointer finger and carried it to the locked window, where she inspected it in the dim light.

An owl charm seemed to swivel its head in her direction.

She flinched but didn't drop it.

"Owls aren't dangerous," Meg told herself and almost believed it.

Lightly, she stroked the engraved feathers on the owl's chest. Nothing happened.

"Okay, good. Maybe the magic has worn off." She laid the bracelet back on the vanity.

Behind her, something crashed into the window. She screamed and ducked behind the bed. A crazed animal thumped against the glass panes with a whooshing sound, and shadows danced erratically on the walls.

Meg peeked over the edge of the mattress.

A huge tawny owl, nearly a foot and a half tall, balanced on the windowsill. Its wings settled against its side, and its head slowly swiveled until its golden eyes found her. It let out a hoot so loud it rattled the glass.

Meg crawled over to the vanity, opened the top drawer, and slid the bracelet inside.

The owl's head swiveled back, and it launched into the night sky.

She slept fitfully that night.

The next day's job hunt was long and fruitless. By the time she got back to the cottage, the sun had set, and Meg's nerves were wound so tight she ached from head to toe. She climbed the steep stairs to the attic apartment and found the door ajar.

"Damn it. Of course, that little thief can pick locks." Who else could it be other than that overly clever Sabine?

Meg cautiously pushed the door open. The overhead fixtures were off. Dim light through the windows reflected off wet footprints headed toward the bedroom. The air smelled fishy. Did the woman take a dip in the river before breaking in?

"If I find you in here, I'll throw you out that window," Meg called out with all the bravado of someone who'd never done such a thing in her life and had no idea how to go about it.

"Talking pretty tough out there," came a familiar voice. A very familiar voice. Valdi, Meg's dead roommate, stuck her head around the door frame to the bedroom. "I'm gone for a couple of days, and you threaten to defenestrate me?"

A hard knot of unused air caught as Meg's throat closed up tight. Valdi appeared hazy as she grinned at Meg with the smile she reserved for the times when she was on the hot trail of a research project.

"Do you know where I left my water-resistant tablet?" The incorporeal Valdi asked as she ducked back into the bedroom. "The one with the long-lasting battery. You know, the one Mom bought me when I moved down here, sure I'd need it when a hurricane blew out our power for a month. As if she expected us to be wading around in ankle-deep water in the rain, emailing her that everything was fine."

Odd request for the recently dead, Meg thought as she followed the specter into the dark bedroom. Reaching the bed, Meg's knees gave out. She sat down hard. Springs squealed in protest. The apparition of Valdi laughed at Meg's stunned silence and sat on the bed across from her, her feet dangling over the side.

"What's up, Megan?"

"You're not dead?" Meg asked. In the dim light from the streetlight outside, Valdi appeared incorporeal, surrounded by a sepia glow. Meg felt like she was seeing her roommate through muddy water.

"I'm gone a couple of days, and I'm dead?" Valdi's grin slipped when Meg didn't respond. "Look, I'm sorry. I should've told you. They took me to the Beyond."

"The Beyond? As in Heaven? Or Hell? Or somewhere else?"

"Come on. I know I should've contacted you before, but it's only been two days."

"Seven. It's been seven days. You were dead. The police came and took your body. Now, you're what? Undead?"

"Don't be melodramatic. I came to tell you I'm okay. I'm just not—" Valdi gestured around the room, "here anymore."

"What do I tell your mom?" Meg croaked around, tears clogging her throat.

How could she explain to Valdi's mother that her daughter appeared as a ghost to say she was fine on the other side? Would they have Meg committed? Should she commit herself?

Valdi sighed in the way she had when she thought Meg was being overly sentimental. "I don't know. Tell her I'm in a better place."

Meg hiccupped. A single sob escaped. "How?"

"You're right. She'd never go for it. You told her I was dead?"

"The police did," Meg whispered, not trusting her voice.

"Best leave it at that, then, if she's already grieving. It's not like I'm coming back," Valdi said matter-of-factly.

Meg snuffled. "Who did this to you?"

"Megan, it's not like that. I was scared, sure. But once I accepted it . . . I can't really explain. You wouldn't believe me. But it's incredible. Better than you could ever imagine."

"Can I come?" Meg asked without thinking.

Valdi's face fell. She cocked her head. "I don't think so, Megan. It's better for you here. Your dream was to live in New Orleans, not mine. You'll be fine without me."

Meg didn't want to die and go to the Beyond. At least, she didn't think she did. But Valdi thought it was wonderful on the other side, and everything here had gone so wrong.

She'd convinced Valdi to move with her. She'd taken her to that bar, and someone had followed them home and killed her. But Valdi's wraith seemed happy, excited even.

"One last place to explore?" Meg asked wistfully.

"Exactly." Valdi's smile returned. "But I've got to go back now. I had to tell you not to worry. And then I thought about the tablet."

"The police have it, along with your laptop and phone," Meg said, confused that Valdi chose to cling to that piece of her life.

"It doesn't really matter, anyway. I'm glad I got to see you again. One last time." Valdi slid off the bed, blew Meg a goodbye kiss, and disappeared into the living room.

Meg waited a heartbeat, listening for the door to the stairs to open and close. When it didn't, she went to look. The living room was empty.

Valdi was gone. Really, truly gone.

All the tears Meg had suppressed came surging out. With a cry of anguish, she sagged back on the bed, letting the reality smother her.

Chapter 27

CARMICHAEL

The light from the bathroom spotlighted Carmichael's note folded on the nightstand. The apartment showed no sign that Thibodeaux had been there since she'd last checked. If he hadn't come home by now, he wasn't going to. Part of her was relieved, but another part had hoped—the part that left this stupid note. She crumpled it and shoved it into the pocket of her jeans.

Carmichael had dropped by her detective's apartment one last time to be sure, after chasing that wretched Sabine across town and losing her. She didn't know how the tiny menace had slipped between her and two officers arrayed around the dilapidated building. She'd circled back and found no way into the derelict building without a crowbar. She'd sent the others home and drove in ever-widening circles searching for the thief.

"Murder suspect," she corrected herself. "Or, at the very least, an accomplice."

Had she known this Megan and the victim before they moved to town? Was this planned? Or had it been a spontaneous murder, Sabine coming in after to help cover up?

Carmichael spit curses as she drove reflexively to the detective's apartment building. She convinced herself that she'd come out of professional courtesy, one officer checking on another, but if she were honest with herself, it was to retrieve that note.

That one sentimental slip up.

It had been long enough. She needed to file a missing persons report on Thibodeaux's behalf. She'd put off the others, saying he was probably homesick, knowing he wasn't. But when he didn't call, that excuse didn't fly. Then she assured them he was too tough to get into trouble. They'd laughed it off at first, but enough was enough.

She had to remove that note before the investigating officers arrived.

Her phone rang, startling her. Before answering it, she scanned the empty apartment, as if someone might have heard and found her there. She took it from her pocket and nearly fumbled it to the floor.

It was Thibodeaux.

"Detective?" Her voice shook. She cleared her throat and tried again. "Thibodeaux?"

"Let me talk. I've only got 3% battery left." It was the detective, his voice raw. She listened as he rasped out instructions. "Get a team to secure Tyler Davis's apartment ASAP. And get the techs back out there for evidence."

"They've been over the whole apartment. You were there." Carmichael let her concern drip through the phone.

"I don't know why, but it's a whole new scene than the one we investigated." Thibodeaux's voice grew tense and clipped, more than just a failing battery. "Report back to me as soon as you get info on the blood and fingerprints."

"Where are you? I'll come get you."

"On my way home. Get people out there, stat."

"You sound rough. Let me pick you up." Carmichael went to the bedroom window and peered out. No sign of the detective yet.

He grunted in answer.

Carmichael's mind whirred, reassessing.

What'd happened to him? What did he think he'd seen? She tried to remain calm.

"Listen. There's a report. We'll go over it when you've recovered." She paused and tried to think of the right words to assuage his agitation. "We were able to close the missing person's report with photos from a traffic cam on the Ponchartrain bridge, showing Davis leaving town in a stolen Camry. We've already sent notices to the surrounding counties."

The line went dead. Carmichael didn't know if he'd hung up on her, or if his battery had run out. She checked the sidewalks from the living room window before leaving. No detective, but something moved fast and low through the shadows. It moved like a dog but looked like a giant cat.

"Or that fox," she said.

It disappeared under the lacy canopy of an oak on the sidewalk. Carmichael waited for it to exit the shadows. Instead, a petite woman with a ponytail emerged, heading for the front door to the apartment building.

"So that's how you got past me."

Carmichael let the curtain drop and headed for the door. The elevator dinged, sliding open as the door to the fire stair closed behind her.

Chapter 28

THIBODEAUX

The slam echoed through the apartment.

Jean-Luc's anger festered. How could he have ever trusted that thief?

He stormed into his bedroom, jerking his suit coat off. The stench nearly choked him. He threw it on the bathroom tile so the smell wouldn't leach into the bedroom carpet.

Sabine never once showed remorse for stealing. She mocked him with it.

He dragged the blood-stained t-shirt over his head and threw it in the garbage.

She dared to show up in his apartment, waiting on him to return, knowing what she'd done.

He tore a clean shirt from the drawer and shoved it shut. It stuck. He kicked it until it fell off the tracks.

She dared to ask him for help. Ask. Him.

He snatched the shirt over his head.

The clever little fox didn't need help.

He paced back into the living room and realized he didn't know what he planned to do there.

Sabine wouldn't ask for help.

Except she did.

Jean-Luc snatched the door open and ran for the stairs. He didn't have time to wait on the elevator.

Outside, Sabine's petite silhouette perched on the curb in front of a fender bender. Horns blared. Drivers yelled.

Had she caused it?

Jean-Luc ran a hand down his face, trying to clear the conspiracies from his thoughts. When he looked up, she was gone. He jogged to the corner and saw her a block down, headed towards the river.

As he caught up, her shoulders visibly tensed. He slowed down and fell into step beside her, panting. A week without real food had left him lightheaded.

"You've never lied before," he said to validate his decision to follow.

Sabine didn't respond. Her slight form remained tight as an overwound spring.

"You needed help?"

No response.

"I was a jackass," he admitted, trying to take the high road despite his concerns. He knew better than to jump to conclusions without all the evidence.

Still, Sabine gave no response.

"Was that the first time you've come by the apartment?" He didn't say *break in*. He thought that was mighty big of him.

"The first time I came by, your girlfriend was there. And then one other time. So, yeah. This was the third."

"Girlfriend?"

"She left a note on your nightstand."

"There was no note." At least he didn't think there was one. Was there?

Sabine shrugged.

"What did you need?"

"Nothing."

"Come on. You wouldn't have mentioned it unless it was something."

She swallowed and blinked fast, but still wouldn't look at him. "A lot's happened since you've been gone. And your girlfriend's not doing a damned thing about it."

"Who is this girlfriend you think I have?"

"You had her frisk me, remember?" Her voice was bitter, but her face looked broken and sad. It shook him.

"Carmichael? She's an assistant. I assure you there's nothing between us. Not only would that be unprofessional, but I don't . . . not Carmichael." Why was he fumbling over an explanation? He didn't owe this thief—Sabine. He didn't owe *Sabine* an explanation.

She shrugged again and turned onto Decatur Street.

"Tell me what's been going on."

Sabine cleared her throat. "Two humans, new to town, wandered into the Faerie Market, got mixed up with a goblin. Ended up in a Fae only club. One's dead."

"And how were you mixed up with these women at the French Market?" He threw out an arm to keep her from walking into traffic. She edged away from him and walked around it.

"Faerie market," she corrected him. So, he hadn't misheard her. "Your girl—Carmichael doesn't know which end is up."

"So, you just took up police work on their behalf?"

"I saw the women at the market. I gave one of them a warning and a pair of earrings so she could see what was going on around her, get scared, and get out of there. Turns out her friend also got a present from a goblin." Sabine snorted. "Never trust a gift."

Jean-Luc ran his thumb over the face of the pocket watch he'd shoved into his pants pocket and reminded himself that Sabine was no murderer. Unless proven otherwise. "So that makes you responsible for finding their killer?"

Sabine stopped just outside the ring of light from a street lamp. They faced the empty French Market pavilion across the street. After a full minute, she said, "Carmichael will tell you there were bloody footprints on the sidewalk outside the cottage where the women are renting an attic apartment."

"And?" Jean-Luc held his breath, fearing the answer.

"They were fox prints."

"Shit."

"Yeah."

Jean-Luc swallowed a string of curses while Sabine studied the empty pavilion, her stance wary and alert. He let out a long, slow breath and asked, "Want to tell me how they got there?"

Sabine shook out her arms and flexed her fingers as if getting ready for a street fight.

"The usual," she said. "I liberated the goblin's bracelet. Must have stepped in the roommate's blood on the way out. It was dark. I didn't stick around to find out."

Jean-Luc found himself mirroring her movements, readying himself for a fight, whether with her or an unseen force. He didn't know.

"You still coming?" Sabine asked in an offhanded manner, but her jaw was clenched, and her eyes narrowed.

"Yeah," he said. "Where is it?"

Her eyelid twitched, and she visibly relaxed a fraction, but still ready for a fight. "You can't see it, can you?"

"No," he said, assuming she saw something more than a dark, empty space.

"Once we're in, you might be able to see the market. Maybe, maybe not." She sounded doubtful.

"I'm not afraid," he said, with memories of the black fog swirling around him.

"You should be." Her breath quickened, and the vein at her temples pulsed hard enough for him to see it. "It might not let you in. If it doesn't, go home. You won't be any use to me."

"If it doesn't, I'll be here when you get out. If you don't show back up within the hour, I'm fighting my way in." His words surprised him. It surprised him even more that he meant them.

Sabine blinked hard and fast. If he didn't know her better, he'd have sworn she was holding back tears.

"You're an idiot."

"Probably," he agreed. Jean-Luc took Sabine's hand, placed the silver watch in it, and curled her fingers around it. "If I don't make it in, wherever that is, ask who's responsible for this."

Sabine nodded, and the watch disappeared into the pocket of her jumper.

"All right then. Come on."

She surprised him by slipping her slender hand in his and gripping hard. She looked up for confirmation. He gave a quick nod, and she led him across the nearly deserted street to the empty market.

As they stepped onto the curb on the far side, a tingle started in his fingertips and ran up his arms. It quickly started to burn, and he resisted the urge to jerk his hand out of hers.

Sabine's grip tightened.

They stepped under the canopy, and a wall of light and sound hit him hard enough to hurt. He shoved ahead as the Faerie Market fought to keep him out. Instead of black fog, he was assaulted by light so bright it sent sparks through his vision.

It was beautiful and horrible.

The light flared like an explosion. A wave of menace washed over Jean-Luc as his hand tore from Sabine's. He was thrown back, landing on the asphalt.

Sabine was gone.

Jean-Luc jumped to his feet and charged, yelling her name. Meeting no resistance, he stumbled to a stop in the center of the empty French Market.

No brilliant light to blind him.

No odd creatures.

And no Sabine.

Chapter 29

SABINE

The apartment sighed as Sabine opened the door. Thibodeaux wasn't there on the other side, waiting to ask why she was picking the lock to his apartment.

Damn him. She needed his help.

Sabine was definitely better at magic, or at least believing in it, than he was. But he just might be better at solving puzzles.

The realization rankled. She threw herself down on his sofa, sinking into the depression where he normally sat. Shoving game controllers aside with her slippered foot, she propped her feet on his coffee table, crossed her arms, and set to brooding.

Sulking in his empty apartment seemed more tolerable than returning to the den she'd arranged for herself in the abandoned townhouse alone. That crooked-assed crow had even deserted her. She wasn't willing to admit that she missed it, or Thibodeaux.

The Faerie market was the next sensible place to look, even though Sabine's hip still ached from her last trip. The bull-headed minotaur said it would open again on the quarter moon. That would be tonight. The gnarled goblin had given Meg the bracelet for some reason. Sabine needed to know why.

"Was he trapping humans on purpose?" Sabine asked the empty room.

She grunted at herself. *Why refer to Meg and her roommate as humans? Did you think you're Fae now?*

"Some people consider witches inhuman," she continued her solo argument.

And what kind of witch do you think you are, with only enough magic to transform into a fox? Sabine supplied a snarky comment for the missing crow.

It was not nearly as satisfying to bicker with herself. Another disservice of both Thibodeaux and the carrion eating crow. But neither was available, so she had to fill in for both.

"Why did you come here?" the missing Thibodeaux asked with his brow furrowed. She liked that look, as if he were trying to fit all the edge pieces of a puzzle together to bind the picture before filling it in.

"Because I didn't want to go to the market alone." The admission tasted sour on her tongue. Luckily, no one was there to hear it.

And because you miss us, the absent crow said with a cocky croak.

"Not true."

A rattle at the door interrupted her thoughts.

Before her instinct to hide could kick in, the door flew open, banging against the wall. Sabine shot off the couch, ready to drop into fox form, when a disheveled bear of a man, vaguely resembling the detective, stomped through the door.

"What the Hell!" a grizzled Thibodeaux growled. A nasty scab ran across his temple. Dark shadows ringed his eyes. A scrappy beard hid the hard structure of his jaw. He wore a wadded suit coat over a damp t-shirt streaked with rusty stains.

Before tonight, Sabine would never have believed that the detective could scare her, but her heart didn't realize this. It struggled to beat its way free and flee this beast of a man that she'd thought she knew.

"What the Hell do you mean, 'What the Hell?'" Sabine bowed up her tiny frame, resisting the urge to fall into fox form and flee with her frantic heart.

"What did you do?"

"I came to check on your sorry ass, and you storm in here growling like a bear?" Now she was mad. Scared and mad. "You've been hiding for a week while I'm out there doing your job because no one else will. You best calm yourself down."

"Explain this?" Thibodeaux threw a hard disk at her. She fumbled it but didn't let the silver pocket watch hit the floor.

If he didn't look so downtrodden and furious, she'd have laughed it off and called it a present. But he was. So, she didn't. Instead, she tentatively asked, "This have something to do with you going missing?"

"Like you don't know."

"I don't know, or I wouldn't have asked." She held up her hands in the universal 'I didn't do it gesture.'

"Then how'd it trap me in that apartment? It had to be some of your magical shit, counting down the minutes until it killed me?"

Killed? Sabine was way too rattled by the word, especially seeing him before her, very much alive and enraged. Had she thought he was dead? The thought of him gone for good frightened her even more than him raging like a beast.

"You actually think I'd try to kill you?"

"You laid that curse on the door and dared me to cross it. You stole that piece of evidence and put it in my pocket, knowing I'd put it back instead of arresting you. It had to have been you. I just don't know why."

Sabine's eyes burned. There was no excuse for her vision blurring.

"I don't kill people, even you."

"What about those dealers that killed your aunt?"

"They lived." Sabine's shoulders ached from the tension. She tried to wriggle it off. "I warned you about the door. I didn't dare you. The watch was a joke. A stupid one, maybe, but just a joke. I've never lied to you, and I'm not starting now. I came here to see if you were okay and to," she stopped and swallowed the knot in her throat, "and to ask for help."

A great roar rumbled from him. He was laughing at her.

"Now, I know you're lying. I'd bet my life, for whatever it's worth, that you've never asked for help once in your life." The scowl on his face wasn't the problem solving one. It was one Sabine had never seen on him before.

Fear melted into something far worse.

"I'm out of here. You need to get your act together. Until you do, I'll continue doing your job for you." Sabine strode past him, slamming the pocket watch into his chest on the way out. "Keep it as a souvenir."

She left, slamming the door behind her.

The burning returned to the corner of her eyes.

It must be rage. Definitely, rage.

She'd come to check on him. She'd even trusted him enough to ask for help. He was right. It was her first time, her first and last. Good thing he set her straight. There was no one willing to help her.

He might look like he'd lived on the streets for a week, but she'd lived there for months, and she was still civil. She didn't bark at friends.

What made you think he was a friend? the missing crow asked.

"Well, you aren't here either, are you?" she barked.

Sabine had made it on her own this long. Not everyone gets a family who cares whether they live or die. Why did she need to care? No one cared about her.

On the street, a screech brought her to a stop. Sabine searched the sky for the ink-black crow against the night sky. She realized the sound was mechanical, not avian, as an ancient Cadillac squealed its worn brakes, stopping halfway into the intersection at a red light.

She was still alone.

As it should be.

Chapter 30

SABINE

Magic washed over Sabine. It nearly knocked her legs out from under her, but she held firm.

Thibodeaux sucked in a sharp breath, and his grip tightened, nearly cracking her bones. He flinched against the fierce light of the market, his eyes pressed shut. He plowed forward as if against storm winds. His arm stretched out, his grip slid, and with a jerk that nearly tore her arm from its socket, the Faerie Market expelled him.

Reflexively, Sabine turned to go after him but stopped herself. She had a job to do. He would be there when she left. He was a man of his word. She breathed in the frizzing energy in the air. If she could feel the magic, she should be able to access it. She'd teach herself if she had to.

For tonight, she need only be aware of the Fae energy surrounding her and not let it ensnare her. Faelight skimmed across her skin, leaving a prickling path behind. Shadows followed, gliding over her, checking Sabine for potential weakness.

"I have none," she hissed, knowing it was a lie.

Maybe Thibodeaux had been right not to trust her. Thieving was a sort of lying, and who trusted a thief?

He'll wait, she told herself. He wouldn't leave until she got out. But if she couldn't get out, he wouldn't be able to break in, no matter how hard he fought.

Winding through the booths of colored silks, striped hides, jeweled lamps, boxes of darkness, caged creatures, trapped wishes, Sabine found the gnarled goblin's booth. It had drifted further toward the treacherous center of the market. The multiple points of her star-shaped shadow, cast by a myriad of lights, drew together like before, pointing toward the dark heart of the market.

"You again," said the goblin without looking up. He knelt with one hand on the table, holding his wares and another reaching deep under it. "Mighty bold. You must be hunting for something unattainable."

He stood up and gave her a sharp-toothed grin. "That's the only reason a thief would dare return to the Goblin Market."

"Faerie Market," Sabine corrected him. He waved her words away. "Why did you give that woman a charm bracelet with no charms?"

"What woman?"

"Warwick, answer the young lady," a deep, soulful voice said from behind her.

Sabine turned, half hoping to find the detective. Instead, the tall man with flaming green eyes from outside the Midnight Jazz Club gave her an assuring smile.

"Are you following me?" Sabine asked accusingly. The goblin cut his eyes between the two of them.

"Yes," the green-eyed man said, surprising Sabine with his honesty. "Zula asked me to keep an eye on you and the tall one. She locked herself in while you led the police on a chase."

"I don't need anyone watching me."

"It looks like you might." He gestured to the bullheaded man barreling through the crowd toward them. Mr. Green Eyes casually cut his hand through the air and the minotaur came to an abrupt halt, bowed, and backed away. To the vendor, he repeated, "Answer her questions."

"As you command, your majesty." The goblin bowed so low that his nose dipped below the table's edge.

"You're a goblin prince?" Sabine asked. He certainly didn't look like any gnarled goblin that she'd ever seen in picture books.

"Prince Pierre III," he introduced himself with the slightest possible bow of his head and pointed her attention back to the vendor. The gnarled goblin forced a smile on his face as she turned her attention back on him.

"You gave the short one my faelight earrings to see the Fae," the vendor told Sabine. "You thought I didn't see that, didn't you? I gave the tall one a bracelet so that she might remember the trouble you'd gotten them into."

He used a lot more snark than Sabine thought was warranted.

"Do you have any further questions for our friend Warwick?" the prince asked.

Sabine looked askance at the gnarled goblin. He was definitely no friend of hers. She withdrew the silver watch from her pocket and dangled it in front of him. "Is this your work?"

"It was one of mine, yes," the vendor admitted without making eye contact. He sorted jeweled rings on a mat as if that had answered her question. Well, it had, but only sort of.

"Who did you sell it to?"

The goblin didn't answer. Ignoring her, he rearranged earrings on the twisted wire tree from which she had liberated the faelight earrings.

Sabine leaned as far across the table as she could to get into the goblin's face. Jabbing her finger back at the green-eyed prince, she said, "He told you to answer my questions."

The goblin looked entreatingly at his prince.

Prince Pierre III considered the vendor thoughtfully. "Warwick cannot give you an answer that he has sold."

"What's that supposed to mean?"

"I sold the answer to that question along with the watch," the goblin said begrudgingly.

The prince filled in the gaps. "If its owner paid for his silence, then Warwick is bound to honor it. He cannot give you an answer that he no longer possesses."

"That's bullshit."

The prince inclined his head. "It might indeed be considered feces in your world. But this is ours, and I kindly ask that you respect it."

"It's actually In Between," Sabine mumbled.

Prince Pierre III gave her a sharp look. She chose not to push the subject.

"Can you tell me if this object has any connection to the young woman who left here with the bracelet and earrings?"

The prince nodded at the vendor, who sneered at Sabine before answering. "I graciously gave the charm bracelet to the tall one so that she could answer such questions for herself. Have her consult it."

Sabine tried to regain her composure, but it didn't work. "I've heard the charms can give dangerous responses as well as memories, depending on the intentions of the giver."

The goblin vendor supplied her with an evil grin. "Did you now?"

"Can the pocket watch be used to trap someone?"

The vendor spread his hands, showing he had nothing more to offer. Sabine searched his nasty sneer and grunted in disgust.

Prince Pierre smiled benevolently at her, which rankled Sabine's nerves. "As the honorable Zula de Bonaire advised earlier, it is time for you to leave the In Between, witchling. It is not safe for one with such little control over her magic. If you remain much longer, I fear the market might decide to keep you."

"I am not a—you know what, forget it. I'm out of here."

With that, the goblin ducked beneath the table, and the prince inclined his head.

Sabine stormed off in the direction that she came but immediately found that her path had deviated. Her steps led toward the center of the market. She rerouted and found that she was once again headed to the middle.

Prince Pierre pointed between a silk vendor's booth and one with swarming butterflies, or at least Sabine thought they might be butterflies. The air beyond the booths rippled. Sabine could make out the warped image of the detective pacing back and forth, testing the air for an entrance.

Once he passed out of her line of sight, Sabine nodded her thanks to the prince, closed her eyes, and darted between the tables before the market rerouted her, yet again.

She ran headlong into what felt like a man-shaped wall and groaned in exasperation. Strong hands caught her. She yelped like a frightened pup, and her eyes flew open.

"Sabine?" Thibodeaux held her at arm's length and looked her up and down, as if to be sure she had not been harmed while out of his sight. Once he was satisfied she was in one working piece, he let go and backed off.

"You waited." She tried to disguise exactly how relieved she was.

"I told you I would," he said rather gruffly.

"But I told you not to." Sabine slipped back into their usual banter, much easier than admitting she was worried that he might have finally given up on her, no matter what he'd said.

"Well?" he asked as the rippling entrance to the market smoothed over and disappeared into the dark.

Sabine handed the pocket watch to Thibodeaux, who took it carefully pinched between two fingers. "The vendor who gave Meg the bracelet also sold that. But he couldn't, or wouldn't, tell me who bought it."

"Couldn't?"

The air beside them began to warp and bulge.

Thibodeaux shoved Sabine behind him, pulled his gun, and took a firing stance.

The protrusion took the shape of a very tall, very wide, and very angry minotaur.

"Run!" Sabine yelled, falling into fox form.

Thankfully, Thibodeaux followed as she darted across the street. But once she'd turned the corner, he stopped. Sabine cursed and ran back to find him facing down the minotaur who had broken loose from the market. The creature barreled across the street. Its eyes locked on hers.

Her muscles thrummed with adrenaline, ready to run, but she couldn't leave Thibodeaux. She shifted back into human form and grabbed for his arm, but he pushed her back around the corner and aimed his gun.

"Detective Jean-Luc Thibodeaux of the New Orleans Police Department. Stop or I will fire."

Sabine popped back around the corner. "You can't just shoot a minotaur."

The creature lowered its head, aiming its horns at her.

"Get back," Thibodeaux hissed at her. He braced his arm, took aim, and pulled back the trigger. "This is your final warning."

The detective took a steadying breath. His finger tensed.

The minotaur charged ahead. Its hoof hit the double yellow line in the middle of the street. And it disappeared.

Thibodeaux started, jerking his finger from the trigger. "Where is it?"

"Gone?"

"Where?"

"Back to the market." Sabine rounded on Thibodeaux as he lowered his weapon and scanned the area. "That was stupid. It could have killed you. Its leash must only extend so far from the market. If it didn't, you'd be—you'd—Why'd you do that?"

After one last sweep of the area, Thibodeaux leaned down until they were nearly nose-to-nose. "Because it was trying to kill you."

Sabine's face flushed hot. "Well, that's just . . . Don't do that. Don't ever do that."

"What?" Thibodeaux asked. "My job?"

She fumed at him for scaring her. For almost getting himself killed. For protecting her when he stood no chance of winning.

Meanwhile, Thibodeaux straightened and searched over her head again for threats before holstering his gun. "If you can see yourself home, I have to clean up and think of an excuse to give in the morning for why I *haven't* been doing my job."

With that, he left her alone once again.

Chapter 31

MEGAN

The melancholy oak let its tremendous branches droop, nearly reaching the ground, except where it had been cut back over the patio. Spanish moss hung in curtains enclosing the space beneath it like a circle of weary wraiths. The candle on the tiled table flickered, bringing the specters to life.

If they decided to leave their watch, narrow their circle, and claim her as one of their own, Meg would not have been the least surprised. She might not even fight them. She moved through her days like a ghost as it was. In the morning, she left to knock on doors, looking for jobs far beneath the level her degree had promised. At night, she secured the deadbolt, latched the windows, and ignored calls from the vanity drawer where she'd stowed the cursed bracelet.

Tonight, she'd given up.

Valdi, her college roommate, her best friend, had been dead for a week and a half. No more than a ghost that had dissipated. Her body was to be cremated tomorrow. Her mother would arrive by noon. Meg was invited to the small family funeral to be held in Chicago the following weekend. The cops had likely given up on finding her murderer. They probably assumed it was Meg, but didn't have the evidence to pin it on her.

It was Meg's fault, after a fashion. It was her choice to move here. Her choice to go out, go to the market. What did it matter what creatures came for her in the night?

Light flared as her joint caught on the candle's flame. The cursed charm bracelet clattered as she withdrew her arm and leaned back in the rusted patio chair. It creaked dangerously but held. She stretched out her long legs across the moss-covered brick pavers and twirled the joint between her fingers. The ember at the end inched toward her nails. She couldn't take her eyes off the light, doomed to die within minutes.

The near silent patter of slippered feet approached from behind, but Meg didn't have the energy to turn, or the will to send the clever little thief away. It had been almost a week since she'd last seen Sabine, and she didn't know how she felt about seeing her now.

Nothing really. She felt nothing.

"Well, aren't you morose sitting out here in the twilight by yourself," Sabine said as she circled and sat in the chair opposite Meg, snagging her joint on the way. She inhaled deeply and leaned back, eyes closed.

"I'm not by myself. Unfortunately."

"Nothing's better than being miserable and alone in the company of someone else, just as pathetic."

Meg grunted in response. "Guess not."

Sabine crossed her arms tight as if she were chilled in the balmy night air.

"Aren't you supposed to be off quizzing goblins and catching murderers?" Meg asked.

Sabine grunted and passed the joint back.

Meg took a long drag from it, crushed it out on the table, then threw the evidence into the weeds just past the oak's massive trunk. The bracelet clattered on her wrist.

"You didn't trash it?" Sabine asked, eyes still closed.

"I tried. It came back."

"Figures."

"Yep."

"Did you ever try them? The other charms?"

"Some."

"And?"

Meg held out her arm so the bracelet dangled between them. Hearing the clatter of the charms, Sabine opened her eyes. She reached out and tapped the star, setting it to swinging. It sparked to life. Flares shot out, whistling and whirring into the tree's canopy. The two women watched, indifferent as to whether the moss went up in flames.

It didn't.

Meg petted the wolf head charm. A blood-curdling howl sounded, echoing throughout the courtyard, coming at them from all directions at once. Sabine looked idly over her shoulder, but no wolf pounced. If it had, Meg didn't think either of them would have moved to save themselves.

When the mournful cry faded, Sabine sat up and dragged the chain around Meg's wrist as if searching for something. Failing to find it, she asked, "No crow?"

"No, but there's an owl." Meg lifted it with the tip of her finger.

Silent wings sent shadows soaring across the circle of light in which they sat. A monstrous tawny owl landed on a low branch to stare at them. Meg half expected to see Valdi arrive, too.

She didn't.

Meg searched her pockets for another joint. She was out. She'd have to visit the man on Bourbon who crouched over his milk crate. He mumbled to pedestrians as they passed, "Weed if you need."

"Good to know," she'd said in response as she walked by on her first day of job hunts. By the third day, she slipped him a ten, and he shook her hand, leaving a snack size baggy with three joints inside. She didn't know if it was a fair trade or not. Didn't care.

"Don't you have a home of your own?" Meg asked, running out of useful conversation. She would have preferred to go back to wallowing in sorrow on her own.

"Yeah. No. Sort of," Sabine said, leaning back and closing her eyes again.

Seeing as Meg wouldn't be alone for a while, she decided she might as well keep up her end of this meager conversation. "That's a pretty vague answer. Sounds like you don't know what you've got."

"I didn't, not until it was gone."

Meg sighed, running out of energy for the discussion already. "And what was that?"

"My aunt left her house to me, but I can't stay there." Sabine paused, presumably waiting for Meg to ask why not, but she didn't. So, Sabine continued without the prompt. "She was murdered there. As far as I know, the kitchen floor is still covered in her blood. The food rotting in the fridge."

Meg cut her eyes to Sabine, who studied her expression. "Yeah, I can see why you wouldn't want to sleep where someone you cared about was brutally murdered. Sucks."

Sabine ignored her sarcasm and went right on complaining. "And my only friend, or potential friend, well, the only acquaintance that remembers who I am, is no longer speaking to me, because he's pretty sure I'm linked to a murder and had him trapped and starved for days."

What do I care? Meg thought, but lacked the will to say it out loud.

"And that pestilent crow who used to follow me around complaining, it just up and left?"

"Would you shut up!" Meg found herself looming over the tiny woman still seated in the rickety metal chair. "What do I care about your missing crow? You think you're the only lonely person in New Orleans? You think you're the only one without a decent place to stay, without bloodstains on the floor?"

Sabine didn't flinch. Her mouth had the nerve to curl up at one edge into a sneer, and she leaned in until she and Meg were nearly nose-to-nose.

"Then do something about it," Sabine hissed.

"What?" Meg yelled back and started pacing the patio.

"Start by asking him," Sabine pointed into the tree canopy.

A young man with tawny skin sat on the limb where the owl had perched moments before. He studied them through thick circular glasses perched on a beak-ish nose.

"Where did you come from?" Meg demanded.

Before he could answer, Sabine asked, "Hobgoblin. Am I right?"

The man nodded in polite response.

"And you can find things?"

Another nod.

Meg crossed the courtyard in two long strides, craned her neck up, and pointed at the man. "If you can find things, then find Valdi's killer." Her voice dripped with venom.

"Respectfully, I cannot," the man said.

"Cannot, or will not?" Sabine rose to confront him, too. Meg was not surprised that this man might be a hobgoblin arriving as an owl. It was no stranger than anything else she had encountered since moving here.

The man bowed her head. "I will answer those questions I can, and will not answer those I cannot."

"Well, that settles that." Sabine threw up her hands in frustration.

Meg rounded on her. "So what? You're just giving up now?"

"No, I say we jerk him out of that tree and make him tell us. They have to. That's what they do. They find things. Are you waiting for payment? Is that it?" Sabine asked, but the man was no longer there.

A shriek preceded the massive owl flying across the courtyard. Its wing swept against Meg's cheek as it disappeared into the night. She tried to follow its path but lost it.

Instead, in the tree shadows stood a man with broad shoulders and a stern face.

Meg and Sabine both gave a startled yelp.

Chapter 32

THIBODEAUX

The Spanish moss trailed down to caress the side of Jean-Luc's cheek as he stepped from the shadows. The sweet aroma of spent weed greeted him. Thankfully, none was in sight.

"Didn't mean to scare you," he said as calmly as possible.

"Thibodeaux?" Sabine asked, looking more vulnerable than he'd thought was possible.

Standing in the shadow cast by the ancient oak, Jean-Luc had listened to Sabine as she listed her losses. Surprised that she counted him as one of them. Did she think he still blamed her for trapping him? Did he?

Jean-Luc had a few days to think it over and decided, against all reason, that he didn't.

"What are you doing here?" she demanded, no trace of vulnerability left.

"Thibodeaux? I know that name." Megan Armand said, more as an accusation than a question, but Sabine answered it anyway.

"He's the detective that would've been on your case if he hadn't been missing," Sabine said, eyes still on him.

"Carmichael's running the case. I'm just assisting," he explained. "She's had officers tailing the both of you for over a week. Those who were able to keep up with you, anyway." The latter, he aimed at Sabine.

"So, you're on a stakeout?" the little thief asked with a snarl in her voice. "Aren't you supposed to do that from a distance?"

Jean-Luc felt his face flush. "I thought I heard a wolf and came to check."

"Whatever. We're fine. You can go back to stalking us from the shadows." Sabine flopped in the chair with her back to him.

"Wait a minute," Megan said, stalling his retreat. "If you're this fancy detective that everyone's been looking for, then get to detecting. Find Valdi's killer."

Sabine spoke over her shoulder. "He already chased off our best lead."

"He wasn't giving you any answers that I could hear," Jean-Luc said, his embarrassment at being caught, turning quickly to anger.

Sabine jumped to her inconsequential height and started barking accusations. "So now you're listening in on our conversations?"

His jaw clicked as it tensed. "That'd be how a stakeout works. You see what you can see and hear what you can hear."

Megan looked back and forth between the two of them as they seethed at one another. "You two have a thing or something?"

"No," Sabine said.

At the same time, Jean-Luc said, "Yes."

Sabine glared at him.

Jean-Luc ran a hand through his hair, then down his face. "We have—*had* a professional relationship. For one investigation. It's over now."

"The relationship or the investigation?" Megan asked.

"Both," he and Sabine barked out at once.

"Good. Then can we get back to mine?"

They both gaped at her. Jean-Luc regained his composure and donned his detective face. How *did* he let Sabine get to him so fast? She smirked, but it looked weak, put on. He thought he could see the pain and fear and loneliness bleeding through.

"Yeah, we can do that," Jean-Luc assured Megan. "I've been reading up on these . . . these creatures. If they're real," Sabine snorted, but he continued. "Apparently, they cannot lie. Maybe she couldn't tell you because, well . . . Let me ask you a bizarre question."

Megan folded her arms around her middle as if to protect herself from the anticipated question and nodded for him to ask.

"You saw the body of your roommate, right?" She nodded. "I don't mean to open old wounds, but I looked into your case. The file says you saw the body as you were led out. One officer said you started screaming as if you'd seen something else. Something that wasn't your roommate, possibly?"

She nodded, closing her eyes.

"What did you see?"

A shudder ran through that tall, lanky frame of hers, and Jean-Luc's instincts kicked in. He guided her back to a chair and sat across from her, leaving Sabine to prowl a circle around them.

Hugging herself, Megan told him how she found her roommate and called the police. How Carmichael had questioned her. And, on the way out, she squinted against the memory. "On the couch, instead of Valdi, there was a man.

Long arms and legs hanging off the cushions. Valdi was short like her." Megan pointed to Sabine. "But curvy and cute and curious. Cute enough that everyone answered her nonstop questions."

"Describe this man to me," Jen-Luc said, trying to gently keep her on track.

She sniffled, then squinted again into the past. "Around my age, maybe a little older, black man with a sort of stylish hipster beard. And there was no blood."

"On the man?"

"Anywhere. It was all gone. Except that can't be right. Because there's still a stain on the floor upstairs. I covered it with a rug a few days ago. If I have to stay, I can't keep looking at it, can I?"

Jean-Luc shook his head. He stole a look at Sabine. Her head was turned, and her eyelids fluttered as if fighting back tears. He thought of the blood still on her aunt's kitchen floor. The police didn't clean up after a murder. They released the homeowner to do it, sometimes recommending a bio-cleaning crew. Only, in Sabine's aunt's case, she was the owner.

He cleared his throat and tried to fit the pieces he had together. Look for the holes. But his mind couldn't help going back to the apartment where he'd been trapped for a week. At the shape it was in when he left. Furniture overturned. Blood across the floor and wall.

Had he been seeing things just like Megan Armand?

When Carmichael went back, she said it looked just the same as when they'd left it. He didn't trust himself to return. And she said the man, Tyler Davis, was caught on a traffic cam leaving town. She showed him the photo.

A young black man with a—

He took out his phone, pulled up an image of Tyler Davis from social media, and passed it to Megan.

She gasped, dropping the phone on the pavers as if it were poisonous.

"What?" Sabine made a grab for the phone, but Jean-Luc beat her to it. "What is it?"

"That's him," Megan said, hiccupping back sobs.

Jean-Luc stood. "Let's go take a look at that stain upstairs."

Not two minutes later, the three of them huddled around the spot. The rug thrown back. The lights on full. Jean-Luc knelt and used his phone's flashlight feature to examine the floor. He ran a hand across the grain.

"It's gone," Megan said, and he nodded in agreement.

"What does that mean?" Sabine demanded.

"It means I need to make a phone call."

He went back to the courtyard before pulling up Carmichael's number. Both women clambered down the stairs after him. He held his voice down in a poor attempt to keep the call private and professional.

"Carmichael, sorry to call so late."

"Do you have something?"

"No, nothing to report at this time. I just had a quick question."

"Are you still at Armand's residence? Did she leave? Do I need to come out there?"

Jean-Luc chose the questions he could answer truthfully.

"Yes, I'm still at the apartment. No, she hasn't left since she returned from another day job hunting." He turned his back to Sabine's scowl and Megan's insulted face. "I just had some thoughts. Has the body, the victim, her roommate, been cremated yet?"

Megan ducked her head into his view and shook it no, mouthing the word "tomorrow."

"Yeah, they cremated the body earlier today. I went down myself to be sure. The parents are due to come tomorrow. And I know if it were you, you would take care of every detail." Carmichael's assurance ran longer than necessary for a simple yes or no question.

"Okay, thanks. That's all. I better get back on watch."

"Stay on Armand," Carmichael demanded.

"I will. I assure you." Jean-Luc moved his thumb to hang up when she spoke again.

"What did you want with the body?" Carmichael asked, sounding unusually anxious.

"Just a wild idea. Doesn't matter."

"It does. You're damned good at this, Thibodeaux. What were you thinking?" Her voice sounded harsh, as if she were uptight about what he might be piecing together.

Jean-Luc trusted Carmichael. He had more reason to trust her than the thief. Yet, he said, "I just thought one more check for wounds might show something."

An audible exhale of relief came through the phone. "I had the examiner go over it twice already. Three times wouldn't show anything new. You're just worried because you weren't there."

Jean-Luc had the impression that Carmichael wanted him to feel guilty about it. Strangely, he didn't. He only felt wary of this conversation.

"You trust me. Don't you, Jean-Luc?" Carmichael asked, using his first name. Everyone on the force used surnames, exclusively.

"Of course, Carmichael," he emphasized the last, before adding, "Getting back to work, I see a light on upstairs."

He hung up and pocketed the phone. The two women faced him expectantly. Both with arms crossed defensively. Oh, boy. Should he kick this hornet nest?

"Go ahead," Sabine said, as if she'd heard his thoughts. "You've got something going on in that head of yours. What is it? And if you think I can be brushed off as easily as that Carmichael character, you're mistaken."

"It would never occur to me that you could be easily brushed off," he said with a sigh.

"Come on," Megan demanded. "Everyone thinks you're this brilliant detective. So be brilliant."

Jean-Luc stretched out his neck first one way, then the other. It certainly felt like a street brawl, and he was outnumbered. He motioned to the chairs.

"Have a seat, ladies. I think we need to finish going through those charms of yours."

Chapter 33

SABINE

Sabine rode in the back of Thibodeaux's car as they passed the Port of New Orleans. The cruise ships had set sail hours before, leaving the closest wharfs empty but for night crews. Then they passed the sparkling lights of the working wharfs.

A train sped by in the opposite direction. Its horn gave a mournful call of warning to them. Paying it no heed, Thibodeaux raced by, headed towards the Audubon Zoo and Park. At Riverview, he turned toward the river, stopping as a security cart approached. He lowered his window, showed his badge, told the guard where they were headed, and asked that he keep any late night joggers away from the area.

A sparse line of trees shielded the park from the inky waters of the Mississippi River. Dim lamp posts marked the walking paths, not meant for use at this late hour. They followed the road through empty parking lots to the far side of the park, stopping near a small pavilion.

Thibodeaux killed the engine and cut the lights. The three of them sat silently, staring through the windshield at the moonlit river. Meg sat in the front with Thibodeaux. Sabine had insisted.

"For the leg room," she'd said. But what she'd meant was, "To give me and Thibodeaux some distance from one another.

Their eyes accidentally met twice in the rearview mirror on the ride over. Sabine made sure it didn't happen a third.

She wasn't prepared to admit how glad she'd been to see him back in the courtyard. The wound on his temple had been cleaned of clotted blood, and a new scab had formed. But the gash had gone too long without sutures. It would leave a nasty scar. He'd shaved, but still had circles under his eyes. His cheeks were gaunt.

"This catfish charm is supposed to bring the killers out?" Sabine asked casually to divert her attention from the detective.

"I don't know." Meg sounded exasperated. "It just gave me the memory of Valdi with this odd couple we met when we first got to the club. Later, she found me to say she was leaving with them. The woman, she was spooky and moody and had a vicious alligator purse. The other person, they kissed me on both cheeks and—"

"And their whiskers tickled. Yeah, I know," Sabine said.

"Then why do you keep asking?"

"To get to the part about him slipping the charm on your bracelet."

"I didn't see him do it."

Sabine searched the walking trail for joggers. "So, Jean-Luc, you think they hauled Valdi back to her apartment to kill her?"

Meg shuddered. Thibodeaux gave her a look of reproach for being so callous, but the way Sabine saw it, they had run out of time for niceties.

"Sitting here repeating ourselves isn't going to help." He checked his holster for his Glock, then got out of the car. Sabine and Meg followed.

"You're bringing a gun to a magic fight?" Sabine asked.

"I'm bringing a Domingue witch," he said. "The pistol is for any alligator bags that try to attack us."

Sabine snorted. "Fat lot of good a witch with no magic will do you."

Meg was not comforted by their banter. Sabine surprised herself by looping her arm through the tall woman's as they marched to the pier. They each jumped the shorter gate. Sabine refused both offers of assistance. At the taller gate, Thibodeaux reached into his back pocket for the short crowbar he'd retrieved from his trunk. Shielding the padlock with his body, he broke a link in the chain, ushered them through, then strung it back into place.

At the end of the pier, Sabine stood with Thibodeaux and Meg on either side of her, feeling like a child between them. The waning crescent moon and smattering of stars reflected off the dark water. The river rumbled as it rushed to the gulf.

"You ready?" Thibodeaux asked Meg over the top of Sabine's head. Jerk.

"No, but I don't expect I ever will be."

Thibodeaux set his feet shoulder distance apart, bent his knees, and slid his pistol from its holster.

Sabine spread her hands to either side, feeling the powerful energy of the river rushing through her fingers.

Meg gave a heavy sigh, then held her wrist over the water, bracelet clattering, and held the catfish charm delicately between two fingers.

Nothing happened.

They waited.

Sabine's fingers vibrated against the current of river magic. It ran through her arms and into her chest. It built until she thought she might burst open.

Still, nothing happened.

Meg shifted and renewed her grip.

Thibodeaux did not move.

Nothing.

Meg dropped her arm.

"Did something happen?" she asked Sabine.

Before Sabine could answer, footsteps approached from behind. They all swung around. Thibodeaux lowered his gun but didn't relax his grip.

A voluptuous woman with thick, heavy hair stalked down the pier on high heeled boots. She held a chain which shone silver by the light of the moon. At the end of the chain an alligator, about three feet from snout to tip of tail, waddled along beside her.

A cruel smile curved the woman's lips. "Percy assured me you'd come, but Leonard and I told him he was a fool."

The rumble of the river amplified to a roar. To Sabine's left, the water crested. A wave swole to twice her height. It sprouted long, whip-like tendrils before splitting into the wide mouth of a catfish. The head of the great fish roiled, composed wholly of river water and magic.

"Percy, there you are. I suppose you were right. The humans couldn't stay away, much as I would have liked them to."

Sabine stole a look at Thibodeaux for reassurance. His 'doing business' scowl was firmly in place.

"Ma'am, you need to come with us to answer some questions," he said in an authoritative voice, remarkably composed.

The woman threw her head back and laughed. It sounded like the cry of a seagull. Sabine had the sudden overwhelming longing to see her feathered friend.

In response, the catfish opened its mouth, and the river's roar turned thunderous.

The alligator rushed at them, straining against the end of its chain. The woman held firm as the reptile's feet scrabbled against the concrete pier.

The water fish rose twenty, thirty feet into the air. Its tail broke free from the river and slammed back down with a crash.

Meg crouched, curling her arms around her knees and ducking her head. Sabine couldn't blame her. It was the only logical move under the circumstances.

"Sabine," Thibodeaux said.

"Yeah."

"I'll cover the female. Can you handle the fish?"

Sabine looked at him skeptically as the woman and fish roared with laughter at their ignorance. Sabine turned to face the river Fae, hands held high, swallowed hard so her answer could pass through.

"Bring it!"

Thibodeaux held up a hand. "Ma'am, I'd like to do this peacefully."

In a quick glance, Sabine took in the sweat dripping down his temple. A bead rolled over the poorly healed wound. His face was stern, but a muscle ticked in his jaw. He cut his eyes to her, giving her a slight smile of assurance.

"You come here for us and beg for me to remain peaceful?" the woman demanded. The once lovely curves of her face sharpened into a cruel mask. "If you want me, come and get me." She dropped the leash, and the alligator charged.

Thibodeaux fired three rounds of bullets. They bounced off the reptile's hide with a ping, as if its scales were made of metal.

The catfish dove. Its mouth wide enough to swallow them all whole. Its waters roiling. The noise deafening.

Sabine braced herself, whispered a prayer, and shoved with all the magical energy bound inside. It blazed in her chest. It singed her arms and broke from the tips of her fingers in arcs of lightning, forming a dome between them and the plummeting head of the catfish.

Awestruck that the currents of magic answered her, Sabine laughed with joy.

The gaping maw met the dome. They crashed together, and her magic sparked. It flared a brilliant blue. Elation ran through her as hot as an electrical current.

As Sabine crowed in triumph, the magic fizzled and died.

The mouth closed over them, dragging them from the pier. Sabine tumbled, thrashing, in the swift current of the Mississippi. Water went down her throat, and the black, unrelenting water pulled her down.

Chapter 34

MEGAN

The water stole Meg's breath, replacing it with death. Her end emerged from the darkness. She tried to relax, to give in, but her body refused. It fought.

Was this how it had been for Valdi in the end?

Just as suddenly as she'd been dragged under, Meg rose on a ferocious wave. It tore her from the river and threw her down on the pier beside the fearless Thibodeaux. The wave culminated in an enormous tail. It flipped at them in a gesture of contempt and smacked the surface of the river, sending another weaker wave to smack them against the concrete.

Meg pushed herself up on hands and knees, retching up river water. Thibodeaux wrapped a strong arm around her shoulders and helped her to her feet. Seeing that Meg was shaken but okay, he searched for Sabine.

The clever woman ran to his side. He reached out to cup her face. His eyes were round with terror. His voice hitched as he asked, "Are you okay?"

"I'm sorry, I couldn't." The bold thief turned her head aside. Her eyes clenched shut. Her face tortured. "I was a fool to think I could protect us."

Except they were saved.

But how?

Howls of laughter from the far end of the pier drew their attention.

The woman from the Midnight Jazz Club with the seaweed hair laughed so hard, she had to be held upright by a person with whip-like whiskers sprouting from under their nose. They laughed just as hard, and their mustaches writhed along as if humored, too.

"Did you see that, Cassandra?" The whiskered person choked out the words. "Did you see the little witchling trying to use her magic against me? It was precious. Just precious."

Cassandra collected herself enough to speak. "Idiotic, perhaps. Precious, it was not. You really have such an odd fondness for these weak humans, Percival. It is a serious failing in your character."

Percival gave her a winsome smile, and she laughed in return.

"Okay, maybe it was just the tiniest bit cute to watch her try. Bless her heart."

"You bless my heart. I'll kick your ass," Sabine barked at them, not realizing she was entirely too tiny to be that fierce.

Meg put a hand to Sabine's chest, holding her back. "Not until I get some answers. What did you do to Valdi?

"Valdi?" Cassandra asked as if the name tasted foul to her.

This time, it was Thibodeaux who held Meg back.

"Cass, don't be so callous. You can see the tall one is clearly worried about her friend." Percival gave Meg an infuriatingly tender look.

"They really are quite tiresome." Cassandra looked around her. "Where is Leonard? You didn't sweep him off the dock with the humans, did you?"

The alligator waddled up on the bank near the end of the pier, dripping river water.

"Poor dear," Cassandra called to it. She gave Percival a sour look, and they smiled innocently back. The alligator scrambled down the pier toward her, butting its head against her calf. She reached down and scrubbed behind its eye ridges. "Don't be grumpy with Percy. You know how they get when they're playing with humans."

Unable to take this farce any longer, Meg tore free from Thibodeaux's hold. She charged the two and grabbed Percy's shirt. She might have tackled Cassandra and thrown her in the river if the alligator hadn't been jealously guarding her.

Unfurling herself to her full height, Meg jerked Percy close enough that spittle flew in their face as she raged. "Forget her damned pet. What happened to Valdi?"

"Oh, dear." The whiskers whipped out to patter at her cheeks, but Meg held tight. "Cassy, can you do something?"

Cassandra folded her arms. "You did ask for it."

"I suppose you are right." Percy cut eyes to the trees bordering the river. "Jokes over, sweetmeat. Your friend seems quite angry. Perhaps you should come out and put her fragile nerves at ease."

Meg didn't understand what he meant until she heard a familiar voice.

"I told you she would not find any of this remotely funny. It's just not her type of humor." Valdi materialized from the tree shadows at the end of the dock and walked their way. "The Fae have a completely different way of humoring themselves. Sometimes it looks quite macabre."

Valdi stopped at Percy's side and cocked her head as if in thought. "Come to think of it, it *can* be quite macabre. Not only the appearance of death, but sometimes actual death amuses them. Fascinating."

Meg could not believe what she was seeing. Surely, this was another cruel trick. Valdi couldn't be alive. She would know. Her best friend wouldn't have let her think she was dead. Sick joke or not, Valdi would have told Meg.

Her ghost had come back to tell her she'd gone to the Beyond.

"Oh," Meg said, realization dawning.

"Do you mind?" Percival gestured to the rumpled shirt still clutched in Meg's fist. She forced her fingers to relax and let go.

"Really, Meg. There was no need for all of this. I told you I was fine."

"She told you she was fine?" Sabine demanded.

Meg hadn't realized Sabine and Thibodeaux had joined her. The detective kept a wary eye on the alligator, but Sabine, hands on hips, scowled at Meg.

"I thought she was a ghost," Meg said.

Sabine hauled back and punched Valdi in the face. Meg's former roommate stumbled back, holding her nose.

"Doesn't look like she's a ghost to me," Sabine said. Thibodeaux looked on, concerned, but did nothing to stop her.

"That one is rather violent," Cassandra said approvingly.

Sabine shifted her glare to the other woman. "You're next."

Thibodeaux subtly shifted his weight until he blocked the woman from Sabine's view.

"Listen, Meg. I'm sorry about all this, but I did tell you." Valdi's voice was nasally and muffled as her nose swole under her hand. "I can't pass up the opportunity to study such an incredible species. You'll just have to get used to the idea that I'm not coming back."

The creatures shared a smirk behind Valdi's back.

Meg ignored it. Her chest ached. It felt like she'd been punched. She cleared her throat.

"I don't want you to come back," Meg said, walking past her once best friend.

"Meg? Meg. What's wrong?" Valdi called after her.

Meg kept walking.

Behind her, Sabine let out a long, curse ladened explanation about what a pathetic friend Valdi was. Behind her, the cursing didn't cease, nor did it lessen in volume. Thibodeaux must have been following her, dragging Sabine along, before the Fae decided to shove her back under the river and leave her there.

Listening to the little thief's diatribe, an involuntary smile tugged at the corner of Meg's mouth even as a tear slid down her cheek. She dashed it away. It wasn't enough, but Sabine's rage on her behalf put the first stitch into the gaping hole left by Valdi.

Chapter 35

CARMICHAEL

The sterile room smelled of alcohol and formaldehyde. Pale green walls gave the room a surreal feel. Arctic air-conditioning blew directly on Carmichael. Her arms, covered with goosebumps, ached from the cold. She refused to shiver as she motioned for the medical examiner to get on with it.

The bodies were already refrigerated. Why did they need to keep the morgue so cold?

The examiner, a stooped man with gray curly hair, checked his chart and located the corresponding number in the grid of doors along the wall. The seal on the door whooshed as he opened the refrigerated chamber and rolled out the rack holding the cadaver Carmichael had requested. The body lay sealed in a zippered bag.

"Thank you. You go make arrangements to have it shipped to this crematorium while I ID the body." She handed him a folder from her satchel with the address for a new crematorium.

He hesitated.

"Is there a problem?" Carmichael snapped. Elderly people made her uncomfortable, and she didn't need any witnesses. He needed to do as ordered.

After a quick quizzing, she'd determined he hadn't seen the body since the autopsy. No reason to. He'd done his job.

Without speaking, the medical examiner gave her a noncommittal nod and left. Once he was gone, the wall of dead took on a menacing air. Carmichael had the sensation that the newly deceased held a seething malice toward her. Images of doors whooshing open, one after the other, and bodies rising accusingly, overtook her for a moment.

She stepped back reflexively.

To counter the chilling sensation, she approached the body with an animosity of her own. She yanked the zipper down to the naval of the subject and jerked it open.

Blood iced over in her veins. She felt it freeze solid in her chest. Her fingers froze as they clutched the bag. Wanting to let go. Unable to.

Instead of the compact figure of a young female graduate, a once handsome man of color stared up at her. His dark brown eyes dead and hostile. His full lips twisted with a vengeance unrealized.

"It wasn't me." She choked on the words.

But he didn't answer.

The missing person, Tyler Davis, lay before her with an empty hole in his chest. His ribs were jagged and broken instead of neatly cut. It looked as if the heart had exploded from its cage. This was not how they handled bodies. The eyes and mouth should be sewn shut, uncaring about Carmichael's guilt. The organs should've been returned, and the chest closed.

With shaky hands, she had trouble zipping the bag over his ragged chest. The zipper snagged just beneath a chin covered in a neatly trimmed beard. She snatched it down and back up where it caught in the carefully styled whiskers. Her chest heaved as she fought a wave of vertigo.

At last, she worked the zipper in place, and ignored the hairs that caught in the zipper. She slid the tray back and slammed the door on the dead.

Collecting herself, Carmichael marched out of the room to confront the reluctant examiner. She was the presiding officer over this case. If she said the body was to be cremated immediately, then he would do it.

She'd stayed awake through the night, developing a plan. Calling all the surrounding crematoriums, she'd found the one willing and able to take the body first thing in the morning. Now, to get the body out of the morgue.

The examiner met her at the desk, face determined. "The family requested to witness the cremation. It is my understanding that they are coming from out of town and won't be here before noon."

So, he didn't process the delivery like she'd told him to.

"You have your new orders. The paperwork is all there. Do your job." His face hardened. Just what she needed this morning. An overly compassionate medical examiner.

He snatched the folder off the desk and picked up the phone. Carmichael waited for him to make the calls and the men to come and move the body before marching out of the morgue and down the chilled corridor. None of this would have been necessary if Thibodeaux hadn't needed to solve another puzzle.

What had he pieced together? He should have just stayed missing.

"Well done," an icy voice whispered in her ear.

Turning in a frantic circle, she searched for the owner of that voice. The corridor was empty. Carmichael picked up her pace, her hard-soled shoes hammering on the vinyl floor. The sound echoed behind her as if she were being chased. Her bravado evaporated.

Carmichael ran as if chased by the damned.

Chapter 36

THIBODEAUX

Jean-Luc followed the signs to the morgue, his temple throbbing. It hadn't stopped hurting, but this morning, it ached as if it were fresh. Must be tension. It comes when you don't trust someone whose word you'd thought unimpeachable.

He'd once felt that way about Sabine. Despite the fact that she was a thief. She was at least an honest thief, if there were such a thing. She did it right under his nose and dared him to stop her.

Why didn't he?

After the inexplicable showdown at the river, the dripping wet Sabine had refused a ride home, walking from Audubon Park, in the dark, alone, at night. And he'd let her. He could've fought her on it. She would have resisted on principle, but he could have. He didn't.

Maybe he was just too tired. Tired of the mystery. Tired of things he didn't understand. Tired of things out of his control. And like it or not, Sabine was all of those things.

A stooped man with gray curly hair sat behind a desk with paperwork spread out in front of him. He looked up wearily as Jean-Luc approached. Carmichael said the body had been cremated yesterday, but Megan said the cremation was scheduled for that morning.

Who did he believe?

"May I help you?" the man asked, removing his glasses and wiping them on his white coat.

Jean-Luc showed his badge as he spoke. "I've come to inquire about a body, a murder victim."

The man's jaw clenched before Jean-Luc could finish his query. He knew which body Jean-Luc had come to see. No, it was not cremated yesterday. Yes, it was scheduled for noon today with the family.

The man gave a disturbing account. "Lady officer comes in here flashing a badge, just like you Detective Thibodeaux," he said Jean-Luc's name as if it had a bitter taste. "She throws around paperwork to rush the cremation. Had the body transferred to another crematorium. Shafted the parents and their wishes. But it's not mine to judge," he said as if it were indeed his to judge.

Jean-Luc's stomach soured. "Can I see the paperwork?"

"She took it with her." The man left Jean-Luc standing at the desk. Before he shut the door behind him, he looked out and added, "You cops need to get your act together. No wonder you get such a bad rap."

Jean-Luc winced but held up a hand to stall him. "One more question. Did you see the body before it left?"

"I closed it up after the autopsy. I'm not a perv. I don't go peaking at the dead for fun," he said and disappeared.

That was drastic, Jean-Luc thought. He felt the disgust, too. The vein under the barely healed wound on his temple pulsed. He'd done what he could.

Not nearly enough.

There was something he could do to set things to right.

Jean-Luc returned to his car. In the front seat sat a stack of old t-shirts used for rags, a scrub brush, and a bucket holding a jug of white vinegar, another of bleach, and two boxes of baking soda. In the trunk was a can of off-white paint, a brush and roller, sheetrock mud, and a spackling knife.

The car carried him across town to the Greenwood Cemetery while Jean-Luc tried to supplement excuses that didn't exist. He sorted through loose pieces of a puzzle he couldn't visualize. Nothing fit.

He parallel parked in front of a cottage with dead ferns fringing the porch. A curious crow sat on the peak of the roof, observing Jean-Luc as he unloaded his car, putting the supplies on the porch swing. On the final trip, he stopped to check out the crow, which looked like any other crow crowding the skies of New Orleans. This one cocked its head, aiming one beady eye at the detective.

"You a friend of the deceased?" he asked, hoping the neighbors weren't watching.

The bird croaked in response, which told him nothing.

Jean-Luc shook his head at his own lunacy and let himself into the Domingue witch's house.

Chapter 37

SABINE

Morning bloomed over the townhouse roofs, setting the clay chimney pots of surrounding cottages alight. Locals walked and biked to work while tourists slept off hangovers. A breeze blew across the city, washing the night's odors out to the river where its current would take them to the gulf.

The bricks of Sabine's hideout grumbled as she wriggled her way out of the loose grate at the bottom in fox form. Once out, she shifted and set the grate straight, wedging it securely into place. She wandered through the cemetery. No longer looking for any lost souls. Ignoring roaming shadows.

A conspiratorial murder of crows launched from their perch on a crumbling crypt. Sabine no longer asked them where her friend had gone. She had treated him poorly when he was left alone after her aunt's death. Now, she was alone, and rightly so.

Occasionally, on her strolls through the French Quarter, she caught a glimpse of Detective Thibodeaux going about his job. To his credit, he didn't evade eye contact. He would nod politely from across the street. In return, Sabine kept her hands to herself and left the pedestrian's possessions in their poorly guarded pockets and purses until he was out of sight.

The break in their odd little tête-à-têtes didn't bother her. She was a thief. He was a cop. Sabine did her job. Thibodeaux did his. And they stayed respectfully on their own side of the street.

The pang just under her breastbone was most likely from hunger. Nothing else.

Stretching out her lithe form, she took in the cool morning air of late autumn. Magic seeped from the bricks, swirled around cast iron columns, and flowed through her fingers, leaving an electric charge behind on her skin.

Sabine shook it off and curled her fingers into fists.

This morning, nearly a month out from her failed attempt to wield magic against the River Fae, she found herself at a pleasant little cottage with a cramped attic apartment. She laughed at the ill fates that had led her here.

Well, she was here now. She might as well let herself in.

*

"You again," Megan Arman said as she entered the bedroom to find a fox sitting in her open window. "Enough of that. Come see my new couch, and I'll make you a latte."

Sabine reverted to her auburn jumper and slippers on size five feet and followed her to the living room. She plopped on the couch and let the stretched woman serve her.

"You get a job yet?" she asked, accepting the amateurly made beverage and sipping it gratefully.

"Yeah." Meg folded herself into an avocado green vinyl armchair. She took a drink and recoiled as it scalded her tongue. After she recovered, she laughed and told Sabine, "Would you believe they hired me at the Sassy Witch? Sells tarot cards, crystals, and witchy t-shirts. I didn't even have to pull the 'I'm friends with a witch' card."

Sabine snorted. "Doubt that would have helped." They sat in a comfortable silence for a few minutes before she asked, "Friends, huh?"

Meg rolled her eyes. "Don't pretend like I don't know why you're here."

"And why's that?" Sabine said with a sly smile.

"You miss me and you're lonely and you want to know if you can take over the other half of the rent and move in with me," Meg said with a smug smile.

"I don't know about lonely. Although I am hungry if you have a croissant to go along with the latte."

Meg gave a sigh of exasperation as if the two of them had been having this same conversation on repeat for years. It felt good.

When she returned with a plate of pastries warmed in the microwave and a half-full jar of preserves, Sabine took in the scent of day-old bread and helped herself. "So, about the rent. From what I understand, the landlords took pity on poor Megan with the brutally murdered best friend and halved it."

"Reading my mail?" Meg said, unsurprised, as she slathered preserves onto a crumbling biscuit. Sabine shrugged. "When you move in," Meg paused to lift her eyes from the jam jar to Sabine, letting her know the issue had already been decided. "Maybe you can start using the door."

"If I did that, they'd figure out you have a roommate. Demand that second half of the rent. And I'd have to get a real job." Sabine jammed the rest of the croissant into her mouth and proceeded to talk around it. "We wouldn't want that, would we?"

"I guess not," Meg said with a devilish grin and held out her chipped coffee mug for Sabine to clink.

The ache in Sabine's chest eased, and she didn't even flinch when a scruffy crow landed on the windowsill and started tapping. This little plan could work out rather well.

Acknowledgements

Here is the place where I thank all those people who put up with me along the way. They're the ones currently hiding behind the sofa, hoping to sneak away in peace. But dear friends, it shall not be. I have put binding spells on the lot of you.

During the writing of this book, Zoë and Sam (proof I'm capable of conjuring awesomeness) passed through like hurricanes and caught me muttering stories to myself. While measuring me for a straitjacket, they suggested I should find some friends to talk to.

So, I did. Writers. The best kind because they are crazy, too.

I am grateful for those who've welcomed me into their writing group, starting with The Knights of Writing under the mentorship of David Farland. Then came the Big Sur Ladies, Wednesday Words led by Jenna Eatough, and the Splinter Faction coordinated by Dustin Adams. And finally, my amazing Superstars family, thanks to Kevin J. Anderson and Rebecca Moesta, and the Troublemakers in the Back Row, students of Dean Wesley Smith and Kristyn Katherine Rusch. Even though my motley crew refers to you as my "imaginary friends," you are real and dear to me.

Two of my fellow creatives in particular have kept me functionally sane and reminded me why I love stories.

Nicole Haskell, thank you for the late-night discussions and irreverent jokes. Your bravery inspires me to crawl out of my spreadsheets and attempt impulsivity (after lengthy analysis and careful thought, of course).

Marie Burghard, your support on this rollercoaster ride of creation has been invaluable. Thank you for teaching me that the act of creating is an act of healing. Your words and art are a balm to my often weary soul.

That brings me to Rob Ashley—Forever and Always. You read every story, most multiple times, and ask for more. You hold my hand when the way is dark. You help brainstorm, listen to convoluted expositions, and still say being married to an author is sexy. Thank you for sharing your story with me and for letting me share mine with you.

About the Author

Julia V. Ashley writes contemporary fantasy, paranormal mysteries, and the occasional peculiar tale, including *Jazz by Faelight: Original Short Stories of Hidden Magic in the Big Easy* and "No Nibbling on the Neighbors," a short story in the anthology *Vampire Survival Guide*. As an architect, Julia finds inspiration delving into the crumbling buildings of the Gothic South where she grew up. She lives along the Natchez Trace Parkway with her husband, a dog-like creature who makes for a dubious familiar, and a varied wildlife roaming the woods.

Connect with Julia
https://juliavashley.com/

Join THE DREAMARC newsletter
https://subscribepage.io/JuliaVAshley-Newsletter
to download a free prequel story.